Let Me Wear Your Coat

John Basil

Let Me Wear Your Coat
Basil, John

Copyright©2012 by John Basil

ISBN-13: 978-1479249718

Printed by CreateSpace, Charleston, South Carolina, U.S.A.

Book design by Dwight Burns

CHAPTER 1

Neil Bricker dug his left index finger into the corner of his right eye, pulled out a piece of sleep crust and gazed blearily out onto the basketball court below. He hadn't seen 7:55 a.m. on a Saturday since the fifth grade, when he'd awaken almost on reflex and sit Indian-style on the floor to watch cartoons, while eating a dry breakfast out of a cereal box. Now, those carefree days seemed as distant as the last year he didn't smear Clearasil on his blemished face.

Normally, nothing short of a crane could lift him out of bed on a weekend before 9:00 a.m. But on the first Saturday of November, 1979 – the opening day of tryouts for the East Hill Regional High School freshman boys basketball team – he was more than willing to lose precious sleep.

Perched on the top row of the school gym's bleachers, Neil took off his jacket and started fumbling nervously with the drawstring of his sweatpants.

"Did you hear what happened in Iran?" asked Neil, turning to his longtime best friend, Jon Bischell.

"Uh-uh," answered Jon. "What's an Iran?"

"It's in the Middle East somewhere. Some guys stormed the U.S. Embassy and took a bunch of Americans hostage."

"When did that happen?"

"Musta happened overnight. My dad heard it on WINS this morning."

"WINS…you give us twenty-two minutes and we'll bore you to tears," cracked Jon, adopting a professional radio announcer's polished, deep voice.

Neil rolled his eyes at his friend's oft-repeated joke and placed his folded clothes in a neat pile next to him on the bench.

"That's what the locker room's for, nerds – it's where the *players* change," bellowed a teenager from center court, bringing all conversation in the gym to a halt.

Startled, Neil looked down to see that the remark came from an unfamiliar source.

"You girls sure you're in the right place?" continued the stranger, who was staring directly at him. "The chicks are practicing in the little gym."

Laughter filled the court and the eyes of nearly two dozen of their peers quickly fixed on Neil and Jon. Neil self-consciously cast his gaze downward, but not before catching sight of his brother, Marc, sitting below, seemingly laughing louder than anyone.

His cheeks turning lobster red with embarrassment, Neil desperately wanted to verbally return fire. But he couldn't pull the trigger. Instead, Neil tried to act as nonchalant as possible, by stretching the blue and white striped tube socks that were already nearly at his knees even higher on his skinny calves, re-tying the laces on his white Chuck Taylors and patiently wait for the wave of insults to wash over them.

"We're not at Eastham Elementary anymore, are we?" whispered Jon to his friend, a silent minute later, after their agitator had turned his attention elsewhere, like a bored grizzly bear, whose prey played dead.

"Ain't that the truth," replied Neil, with a slight shake of his head, as he fruitlessly tried to dry his cold and clammy hands by wiping them on his cut-off jean shorts. "Man, I didn't think there'd be so many kids – and tall ones – at tryouts, did you?"

"Don't worry about it. We were in the starting five at Eastham last year."

"Yeah, but except for shooting around in your driveway, we haven't played at all since last winter."

"But we *never* play basketball in the summer or fall. We're always playing baseball or chucking a football."

"I know, but look around. Most of these kids are from Woodbridge. Who knows how good they are? I'm just saying, we have more competition now than we did at Eastham."

~~~

At 8:00 a.m. sharp, Coach Jim Preece strode into the gym. Muscular, tall and bouncing quickly on the balls of his feet, he was trailed by George Krotzen, his lanky assistant, an East Hill baseball cap tugged snuggly over his prematurely balding head.

"Huddle up, guys," said Preece, gesturing to the bleachers in front of him. "This is some turnout. For those of you who don't know us already from freshman football, I'm Coach Preece and this is Coach Krotzen. Like you, we're new to East Hill, but we've coached all over. I've been a football, basketball and baseball coach in schools in Jersey for the last ten years and prior to that, I

spent two seasons as an outfielder playing "A" ball in the
Baltimore Orioles' chain. Coach Krotzen has also coached at high
schools in the state. Most recently, he was the jayvee baseball
coach at Garfield High.

"Now, as far as our schedule goes, over the next two weeks,
we'll be practicing every day but Sundays. Today and next
Saturday, we'll go for two hours. On weekdays, we'll practice for
ninety minutes after school, from 3:00-4:30.

"We'll have two cut-down days. The first, will be next Friday
and the last'll be the following Friday, where we'll get down to our
twelve-man roster. Any questions? No? Okay, let's get to it.
According to the sign-up sheet, there are thirty of you here. I
recognize some faces from the football team...Mr. Thorne, good to
see you...and we'll learn the rest of your names as we go along.
But for now, to help I.D. you, we'll assign you numbers to wear
on your shirts. As I call out your name, come down and pick up
your number. Argello...Bischell...Bricker..."

After stretching exercises and a few warm-up laps around the
court, Preece and Krotzen put the freshmen through a series of
ball-handling, shooting, rebounding and defensive drills. In
between, the coaches mixed in dreaded "suicides," in which the
players were required to sprint from one end line to the nearest foul
line and back, to half court and back, then to the far foul line and
back, and finally from end line to end line.

Neil fared well in the shooting drills. Ever since he was strong
enough to push the ball overhand, Neil had an uncanny ability to
make shots. Catch and shoot, off the dribble, mid range, bombs,
from the corners, wings, foul line, or the top of the key, shooting
came easy to him. It was the *one* true basketball skill he excelled
at.

4

But ball handling was another story. A year earlier at 5'8", Neil had the size to play forward on his middle school team. Consequently, Neil let his dribbling skills atrophy, concluding he wouldn't need to develop them at his new position. By the time Neil enrolled at East Hill, however, it'd been eighteen months since he'd grown a centimeter. Still, with above-average athleticism and a keen shooting eye, Neil assumed he'd be good enough to earn a spot on the freshman team – regardless of his ball handling deficiencies. Now, though, as Neil stumbled his way around the orange traffic cones set up on the court for dribbling drills, he feared he might soon pay the price for his teenage hubris. And echoing loudly in his head were the words of his father – uttered countless times the year before – *"I'd work on your ball handling, if I were you. You won't be able to get by on just your shooting. Height isn't in your genes, so you can't expect to be tall for long."*

"Take a seat, number three," barked Coach Krotzen, pointing his pen at Neil, then jerking his thumb, before scribbling a note on his clipboard, after the youth had a ball taken away from him during a dribbling drill.

Physically and emotionally spent, Neil slumped to the sidelines. Sitting alone on the floor with his back propped up against the cold, blue padding that lined the gym walls, he ran a clean towel over his face, wiping away perspiration that was equal parts flop and physical-exertion sweat. Watching the rest of his group complete the drill with relative ease, Neil knew his father had been right.

Neil thought of the thick booklet of basketball drills his father gave him and Marc several months earlier to help them prepare for their impending tryouts; the manual whose spine had never been cracked. The one that was collecting dust on his desk, under the unworn, engraved silver bracelet – now doubling as a paperweight – that he'd received from a clueless relative the previous Christmas.

It was too late to do anything about it now – as his father often said, "coulda, woulda, shoulda," whenever Neil voiced displeasure over a missed opportunity. Expelling a deep breath of air, Neil looked up to the ceiling at the half dozen championship banners hanging from the gym's rafters and came to the sobering conclusion that his game, like his height, had apparently peaked.

~~~

"Bring it in, guys," said Preece, after blowing his whistle and waving the boys to center court when the ball-handling drills ended. "For a first practice, that went pretty well. A lot of you have obviously been working on your games. Okay, see you Monday at 3:00."

"I'm glad that's over with," sighed Jon, ten minutes later, stepping outside into the sun-splashed warmth of an unseasonably hot late-autumn day. "I was more nervous for this than I was on the first day of school. What'd you guys think?"

"We've gotta lot of talent," Marc answered, meticulously styling his short, spongy black mane with a hair pick. "I think we'll have a good team."

"I got on a hot streak at the end of the last shooting drill," said Jon, removing his windbreaker and tying it around his waist. "Musta made eight jumpers in a row."

"Who called us nerds?" asked Neil to Jon, finally contributing to the conversation.

6

"Bobby Thorne," answered Jon. "He's from Woodbridge. Jerk's..."

"That figures," cynically interrupted Neil. "I'd have heard about him if he'd moved to Eastham over the summer."

"He's in my English class," continued Jon. "I'll bet you he's already made the team, because the coach knows him from football; I think he was the starting QB."

"Yeah, he was," added Marc. "Thorne's really not that bad once you know him. We sit at the same lunch table and we have the same history class; he's a funny dude. Last week, he snatched some kid's beanie off his head and played keep away with it."

"Beanie? You mean, yarmulke?" asked Jon.

"Yeah, that was it," said Marc.

"Sounds like a regular Steve Martin," said an unimpressed Neil, sarcastically. "I noticed *you* thought he was funny when he busted on us today."

"Well, it *was* funny what he said," answered Marc with a shrug. "I don't know why you didn't change in the locker room with everyone else."

"Forget about him," said Jon to Neil. "We have enough to worry about trying to make the team."

"That won't be a problem for you guys," shot back Neil. "You'll both make it. Marc, you're already talking about the team like you're a part of it. The way I handled the ball today, I'll be lucky to get past the first week of cuts."

7

"So what?" Jon replied. "I didn't do so well at those either."

"But you don't really have to worry about that," responded Neil to his 6'0" friend. "You're a forward. How's a guard, who can't dribble, supposed to make the team?"

"If it's bugging you that much, then why don't we play this afternoon?" asked Jon.

"Not today," grumbled Neil. "I'm too tired."

"Hey, what's that Krotzen's problem?" asked Jon. "He was yelling at everybody. The head coach didn't even yell as much as he did. I thought he was gonna make this one kid cry, he was riding him so hard."

"It didn't look like he yelled at the kids who played freshman football very much," replied Neil. "He was joking around with them."

"That figures," said Jon. "Football players run this school. They get all the breaks. Hey, wasn't Gerry gonna be a football player for Halloween this year?"

"No, he was a hobo, instead," said Neil.

"Just like you used to dress up as, Brick," said Jon with a laugh. "You musta been a hobo like five Halloweens in a row."

"You think my folks would *ever* spend money on costumes?" asked Neil. "It was always an easy costume to make – I'd just borrow some of my dad's old paint clothes."

"You shoulda come out with us on Cabbage Night," said Jon, turning to Marc. "We TP'ed a lot of houses and trees really good this year. It was frickin' awesome."

"No way," exclaimed Marc, shaking his head. "I haven't gone out on Cabbage Night since the year that cop almost took a shot at me, remember that? I was crouching next to a garage, holding a can of shaving cream and he drove by and thought I was breaking in. Shit, he knows kids are gonna be out the night before Halloween doing stuff and I *still* get hassled. Who knows what would've happened if you guys hadn't come around from the house next door in time to take the heat off me."

"Later," Jon said, as the threesome reached the street where he turned off toward his home. "Brick, let me know if you change your mind."

"Later," answered Neil and Marc in unison.

CHAPTER 2

"How was practice?" greeted the boys' mother, Ann, who, judging by the squeak of the rusted hinges on the back door, didn't need to look up from loading the last of the breakfast bowls into the dishwasher to know that her eldest sons were home.

"Pretty good, mom," answered Marc cheerily, pulling off his sweatshirt.

"Fine," muttered Neil unconvincingly, tossing his jacket onto the overflowing coat rack and opening up the refrigerator to remove a quart of Tab, his mother's favorite diet cola. Pouring himself a drink, Neil was too thirsty to wait for the head to settle and downed the foamy contents in one gulp. After refilling his plastic cup, he returned the soda to the fridge.

"Where's dad?" Neil asked his mother, wiping the froth from his peach-fuzzed top lip with a bare forearm before polishing off his second drink.

"He's in the parlor, doing some paperwork."

Not wanting to tell his father how poorly he'd played, Neil put his empty cup in the dishwasher and stealthily began to creep up the flight of stairs to the second floor.

"Who's that? Neil? Marc?" asked Al Bricker from the parlor, hearing Neil's creaking footsteps on the bare wood staircase.

"It's me," admitted a resigned Neil, who was only steps away from a clean getaway.

Trudging down the stairs and through the butler's pantry, Neil found his father stretched out on his favorite recliner, surrounded on three sides by spilling mounds of manila folders. An economics and history teacher at a high school just over the border in southeastern New York, Al was immersed in the same Saturday morning ritual he'd engaged in for the past twenty years: Preparing lesson plans for the week ahead.

Well read and articulate, at parties Al could contribute insightful commentary at the drop of a cocktail napkin on any number of subjects, but sports were his true passion. A former football letterman at the University of Vermont, Al claimed he could tell a lot about a man by who his favorite teams were and even more about him if he didn't care for sports at all. Sports were embedded in most male's signature Y chromosome, he said, so there was something unnatural and a bit off about men who didn't at least have a passing interest in athletics. While a sports fan could damn well be an ass in Al's book, one who wasn't a supporter at all had two strikes against him – and probably no balls.

Of all the Bricker kids, Neil took to sports the most – athletics being the common thread that wove through his and Al's father-son relationship. The two spent many nights and weekends together watching sporting events on TV. Oftentimes, the only noise that passed between them would come from the family's old black and white thirteen-inch, rabbit-eared set, and yet, Al and Neil were convinced they were spending quality time together.

Al's favorite teams became Neil's, the two referring to their clubs as "we," as if they had a financial – as well as an emotional – stake in them. Father and son's moods hung on their teams' fortunes; a win made their day, while a loss had the power to ruin even inherently joyful events like a birthday, Christmas or the last day of school.

"How was it?" asked Al, when Neil entered the room, looking up from behind a heap of papers and pushing a pair of scratched reading glasses towards the bridge of his nose.

"Okay," said Neil. "There's a lotta kids trying out for the team."

"Isn't that what you expected? Competition from Woodbridge boys?"

"Yeah, I guess."

"What kinda things did they have you do?"

"You know, the usual: Shooting, dribbling, running."

"And how'd you do with those?"

"Good."

"I bet they'll put you at point guard. How was your ball handling?"

"Not bad."

"Uh-huh."

When it came to lying, Neil knew he was more transparent than a piece of Cling Wrap. If ever he tried to get away with something and was administered a polygraph test, the machine would undoubtedly combust under the weight of his deceit, its needles flying wildly off the spreadsheet. Still, despite sensing his father's skepticism, Neil didn't flinch.

"How'd Marc do?" asked Al, figuring he wasn't going to pry any more information out of Neil about his son's practice performance.

"He thinks he did good. Hey, anything going on with the hostage situation?" asked Neil, eager to change the subject, even if he wasn't particularly interested in the answer.

"No. It's at an impasse. The Iranians want the U.S. to send the Shah back so he can stand trial; Carter's not gonna cave to those demands."

Fifteen seconds of awkward silence passed before Neil broke the ice with his second consecutive lie.

"Well…I've got some homework to do," the teen said.

Walking upstairs, Neil ascended one more flight to the attic bedroom he shared with Marc and Gerry. Craving privacy, Neil was relieved to find the room empty for a change as he hurled his body onto the top cot of his and Gerry's bunk beds.

With no intention of doing homework, Neil stared blankly at the ceiling, pondering his short-term future and turning the day's events over in his head. As if doing it often enough would somehow produce a better outcome.

An indifferent student, Neil knew that he wouldn't be able to channel all his energies into academics, if he didn't make the basketball team. Neil had little interest in Math, except when he used it outside of the classroom to calculate baseball batting averages or earned run averages. And he didn't like to read, unless the subject was sports. Neil's idea of literary classics were the stacks of yellowing *Sporting News* he kept piled high in his clothes closet.

Neil expressed himself through the physical acts of playing sports. The only thing separating him from the average wimp, he knew, was his athletic ability. If there was any such thing as being a wuss *and* an athlete, then Neil fit the profile to a T. He was a sports anomaly, the accidental competitor.

Turning over onto his stomach, Neil's eyes changed from blank to intense, recalling how Thorne had humiliated he and Jon in the gym that morning.

"I shoulda done something to that ass," Neil mumbled quietly. "Why didn't I do something? *Anything?*"

Neil stewed a few seconds more, before a half smile creased his face, realizing he was kidding himself into believing that any action he could have taken would have stopped the bullying. Gandhi was more confrontational than Neil. Plus, the well-built Thorne easily outweighed the 115-pound Neil by forty to fifty pounds.

"Neil, dinner time!" shouted his mother from the bottom of the attic steps.

Already? Neil wondered. Tilting his head off the pillow, Neil looked down at the Quartz alarm clock radio on his desk, now glowing 5:02 in the gathering darkness of his room.

Arriving after everyone else had already taken their seats at the kitchen table, Neil took his customary spot next to Gerald (Gerry), the baby of the family. Across from him sat his fraternal twin, Molly, and at her right, Marc. At the head of the table sat Al, with

Ann at the foot. These were the family's "assigned" seats. The ones they'd settled into years ago. Sitting anywhere else now at the table would be as strange to them as trading beds.

Still stewing over his poor performance at the tryouts, Neil picked at his lukewarm plate of meatloaf and Birdseye mixed vegetables and gladly allowed the other kids to carry the conversation. Amidst the obligatory dinnertime noise – the competition of one sibling trying to talk over another and Gerry's inevitable spilling of his glass of milk – Neil could always count on his family being distracted enough so he could be left alone.

"Marc, honey, slow down," Ann cried, "you'll get sick eating so fast."

"Can't help it, mom," said Marc, who'd already wolfed down one slice of meatloaf and was now stabbing his fork at another from the platter on the table. "I'm starving."

"Worked you pretty hard in practice, huh?" asked Al, with a knowing smile.

"Yeah, it was tough," answered Marc. "But it woulda been harder if I hadn't been playing in those pickup games you said I should play in. Good call, dad."

"That's the only way to get better – by playing," answered his father.

"Speaking of playing," said Ann, "is anyone up for a board game after dinner – maybe Yahtzee or Scrabble?"

"Can't, mom," Marc replied, between bites of his dinner. "Going out."

"Me, too," chipped in Molly, a dead ringer for Dorothy Hamill – right down to the Olympic figure skater's signature bobbed hairstyle.

"Oh, that's right," Ann said, sarcasm dripping from her mouth. "It's Saturday night. What was I thinking? Well, we can play with three then."

"Three?!" exclaimed Gerry. "But two minus six is four, mom."

"That's right," Ann said in agreement. "But y*ou'll* be going to bed right after dessert, young man. I was speaking of your father, myself and *Neil*, unless…he has plans, too."

"No," mumbled Neil. "Jon's sleeping over at his cousin's house."

"You know, there *are* other kids from school who you could do things with," said Ann.

While Molly and Marc's social calendars were usually full on Fridays and Saturdays, Neil's weekend evenings were no different from his school nights. If Neil wasn't at Jon's house watching a ballgame on TV, then he was at home, tuned into *The Love Boat* and *Fantasy Island*. Neil was basically a shut-in – and his non-existent social life continually drew his mother's attention.

~~~

When practice resumed the next Monday, the swarm of butterflies that had been nesting in the pit of Neil's stomach all weekend took flight. Playing uptight and afraid to make mistakes, he did just that.

Once more, dribbling remained the Achilles Heel that rubbed on the back of Neil's cheap high-tops. And now he had a new

16

problem to worry about. Neil's unfailing shooting touch mysteriously deserted him and almost every non lay-up he took that day badly missed its mark. The only thing he did right was change in the boy's locker room before practice, thereby avoiding being called out again by Thorne.

"I don't think I could've played any worse today if I tried," said Neil, angrily flinging open one of the glass and metal doors at the school's entrance with such force that it quickly snapped back at him before he could exit. "I'm gonna get cut for sure."

"You need to chill out," Jon said, brushing his long blonde hair, parted down the middle, out of his eyes. "It was only the second day of practice, for crissakes! You've got at least three more days to prove to the coaches you belong on the team."

"You weren't the only one," added Marc, casually squirting a mist of Binaca breath spray into his mouth. "I don't think I played as well as I did on Saturday."

"I wouldn't be surprised if they cut me before Friday," lamented Neil."

"It's done, forget about it," advised Jon. "Do you wanna come over tonight after dinner and shoot around. Marcus…sorry…Marc, you can come over, too, if you want."

"Not tonight," answered Marc. "I've got a big Math test to study for tomorrow."

~~~

Shortly after supper, Neil zipped up his gray, hooded sweatshirt, pulled a woolen New York Jets knit cap tightly over his head and started out for Jon's house. By the normal sidewalk route he could

17

make it there in about ten minutes, but Neil often shunned that option in favor of a more direct path that cut his travel time in half. To anyone who was unfamiliar with the terrain, this course – especially given the absence of streetlights – would be tricky to navigate. But Neil had made the commute so often, that he'd carved his own footpath in spots.

Hopping the nineteenth century stone wall that lined the rear of his family's property, he headed west, trespassing through a neighbor's backyard, up a short, gravel incline and then over the railroad tracks. After fording a creek, Neil turned left and followed a narrow dirt trail that led behind the houses on Allen Street. Two minutes later, he parted a row of hedges, covertly slipped onto the lawn of a home on New Street, ran to the front and then crossed the road to Jon's house. Jogging up the tree-lined driveway, Neil heard the sound of a basketball bouncing on pavement. Coming from inside the garage, Neil recognized above the static strains of an old transistor radio the familiar voice of New York Knicks radio play-by-play man, Marv Albert, calling the waning moments of the first half of a game against the NBA's Atlanta Hawks.

"Six seconds left...Sugar Ray crosses the center stripe, guarded closely by Johnson...he switches to his left hand...four seconds to go...and dribbles along the left baseline...two seconds...Richardson passes to Williams open at the top of the key...one second...he pulls up with Furlow's hand in his face...at the buzzer...YESSSS!"

"Who's winning?" asked Neil, emerging from the shadows onto the spotlight-drenched driveway court.

"Hawks by four at the half," answered Jon, greeting his friend with a one-handed bounce pass to the chest.

18

"Knicks'll lose," said Neil, catching the ball then stopping to set his feet and launch a twenty-foot jumper that clanged off the back rim and shot high above the backboard. "They don't have no one to guard Drew and Roundfield."

"Don't have 'no one?!' Nice English. You mean the *great* Toby Knight and Larry Demic can't do the job?"

"Those guys are lucky to be in the league. Holzman should start Meriwether and Sly Williams instead of them."

"Gimme a break. Neither of those guys can shoot or board."

"Too bad Earl the Pearl's on the injured list. The Knicks need his scoring off the bench," Neil said, spontaneously breaking out the legendary Monroe's patented spin move before laying the ball in softly off the backboard.

"Do Cartwright's free throw," demanded Jon, returning the ball to Neil with a knowing smile of what was to come.

Positioning himself some fifteen feet in front of the hoop, Neil set his sneakers shoulder-width apart. Then, in a perfect mimic of the Knick rookie center's unorthodox shooting form, brought the ball high over his head as if he was making a circle with his arms. Pausing, he cocked the ball in his hands slightly to his left, bent his knees and with elbows flaring out, uncorked his body and flicked home a perfect swish.

"How can he shoot like that?" laughed Jon, catching the ball off one bounce and dribbling it out from the basket.

"I dunno," shrugged Neil, "but he's hitting almost eighty percent from the line; he's the Knicks best player right now."

"No way. Richardson's better. He'll make the All-Star Team this year. You watch."

"What?! He averaged six points a game last year. He was terrible."

"But he's been playing well this year. Plus, he beat out Jim Cleamons for the starting lead guard spot."

"Big deal. My mother could beat out Cleamons."

The two proceeded to take turns challenging the other to imitate the shooting strokes of their favorite players. Only the broadcast of an inane Manufacturers Hanover commercial, starring comedic actor Tim Conway, broke their concentration.

"Whenever my dad hears this," Neil said with a laugh, "he always asks 'Who in his right mind would use a line of credit to pay for *basketball* tickets?'"

When the boys ran out of players to impersonate, Neil and Jon transitioned to their natural shooting styles. Without the pressure of tryouts weighing him down and with the resumed Knicks game providing the soundtrack, Neil played loose and relaxed. Making his way around the half court, he began fluidly pumping in jumpers from all points, angles and degrees of difficulty. Progressively expanding his range along the perimeter, Neil moved as far as he could along the square-shaped driveway, until he was routinely hitting shots from some twenty-five feet away.

Never mind that the night temperature had fallen to under thirty degrees, causing the tips of his fingers to grow numb. Or, that the three layers of clothing he wore on his upper body constricted his arms. Neil was in a shooting zone. He could have made those shots wearing oven mitts on his hands.

~~~

"Time to come in," yelled Jon's mother from the back door, an hour later. "Your brother can't sleep with that ball bouncing."

"Okay. I'll be right there," Jon answered. Turning to Neil, he skeptically asked, "See you at the corner at 7:30 tomorrow?"

"Of course," said Neil, stuffing his ice-cold hands down the front of his sweatpants to keep them warm. "Aren't I always there on time?"

"I'm serious, Brick. I've already been charged for five tardies this semester because of you. And today, you didn't show up until 7:40."

Jon paused, recalling with a laugh the scene that morning when he spotted his friend's skinny, corduroy-covered legs churning fast in the underpass in a futile attempt to make up for lost time.

CHAPTER 3

Neil returned home via the same shortcut, running all the way. The woods were now almost pitch black, the only light coming from a harvest moon. Although Eastham was the kind of suburb where "crime" amounted to motorists who might go thirty-five miles per hour in a twenty-five-miles per hour zone, the violent images of *Halloween*, seen a week earlier on TV, were still fresh in Neil's mind and he didn't want to give any potentially lurking serial killer a chance to jump him. Sprinting along the path, hyper sensitive to any sudden movement, Neil's eyes darted and squinted intently so as to avoid veering off and into any low-hanging branches; his vision further clouded by the condensation from his cold breath and the stinging smoke from a nearby leaf burning.

As much as Neil didn't like traveling this route alone at night, he was glad Marc had declined Jon's invitation to join them that evening. Running scared by himself through thick woods in the dark was still preferable to being in the uncomfortable company of Marc.

Bursting safely through the back door, Neil hung up his sweaty knit cap on the coat rack and peeled off his sweatshirt and tossed it over a kitchen chair. Tugging open the perpetually stuck refrigerator door, he poured himself a tall glass of powdered milk – the consistency of latex paint – and chugged it before walking into the parlor to find his mother and father sitting in front of the TV.

"Did you lock…," began Al, stopping in mid sentence to cover a yawn with his forearm, "…up the house?"

"Yeah," replied Neil, still breathing heavily from his run.

"I'm going up. Goo—ood night all."

Neil stretched out on the floor and pulled off his scuffed and faded blue and white Puma sneakers. "What're you watching?" he asked his mother.

"Nothing. Your father was watching a basketball game. You can turn it off."

"Who won? The Knicks? The score was close when I left Jon's."

"You're asking me? I dunno…I think the Birds won."

"You mean the Hawks?"

"Hawks, Birds…same thing. Say, it was nice to see you and Marc come in together from practice today. Are you seeing him more at school now?"

"Not really," said Neil, fidgeting with the laces of his sneakers.

"Maybe you could go out with him on the weekends, so you can make some new friends," Ann suggested. "I'm sure he'd love for you to come along."

"Are you serious? I'm not going to invite myself. How desperate is that?"

"It's not desperate. Jon's always been a great friend to you, but don't you wanna meet new people now that you're in high school? Marc and Molly love East Hill; I'd like you to be as happy as they are."

"Oh, sure. Maybe I could join the cheerleading squad with Molly."

"Don't be smart. You know what I mean."

"But it's easier for them to be popular and make friends."

"That's why I'm saying: ask Marc if you can tag along with him and his friends to the movies or wherever. If they like him, why wouldn't they like you? You're brothers."

"Get real, mom. We have different last names, so it's not like anyone can tell we're related. And in case you hadn't noticed, we don't exactly look alike."

"Well, I don't think it's such a bad idea. Think about it. I'm going to bed. Don't stay up too late. And don't wake up Gerry."

Ann kissed Neil on the top of the head, tousled his wavy brown hair and ascended the stairs to the second floor.

Left alone, Neil's mind wandered to his life before high school. Before he was thrust into a new school, with new people; back when he knew Marc as Marcus. If high school was *really* supposed to be the best time of Neil's life, then he was profoundly fearful of what lay in store for him after he left East Hill.

Snapping out of his daydream when the clock on the mantle above the fireplace chimed announcing the 11:00 hour, Neil walked upstairs to get ready for bed.

"Who's in here?" whispered Neil, knocking softly on the kids' closed bathroom door.

"It's me," said Molly. "Give me a few minutes."

"C'mon, Moll. You're never just a *few* minutes. I wanna go to bed. Let me in."

24

"No, Neil. Wait your turn."

"I'll be done before you know it. I just need to brush my teeth."

Without saying a word, Molly unhooked the latch on the door.

"That wasn't so hard, was it?" asked Neil, entering the bathroom and quickly proceeding to smear a glob of Pepsodent on the bristles of his well-worn toothbrush.

Brushing furious and sloppily, toothpaste was soon foaming out of his mouth, running down his forearm and dripping into the sink.

"Three out of four dentists surveyed say that's gross," said his sister with disgust. "Are you sure you couldn't have done that any faster?"

"It's my new speed record," said Neil, spitting out the toothpaste.

"You must be *so* proud, doofus."

Ignoring the putdown, Neil left the bathroom and climbed the attic steps two at a time to his bedroom loft. Stripping down to underpants and a t-shirt, he tossed his dirty clothes one at a time towards his drum kit set up in the far corner of the room – his sweatshirt landing on the snare and the pants impaling the top of the high-hat cymbal stand. Feeling around in the dark for the end of his bunk bed, Neil scaled the footboard (he never used the ladder) and hoisted himself on to the top bunk. His spirits buoyed by a night out shooting hoops, Neil soon dropped off to the most satisfying sleep he'd enjoyed in days.

~~~

Running late the next afternoon from their fourth-period classes, Neil and Jon were unable to find an open table in the crowded cafeteria. After two unsuccessful loops around the room, they noticed two available chairs at a long table occupied by Marc, Bobby Thorne, and some of the Woodbridge kids, who they recognized from tryouts.

"Let's sit there with Marc," said Jon, pointing his brown paper lunch bag at the table.

"No, let's keep looking," answered Neil, peering over Jon's shoulder at the table and shaking his head. "Something will open up eventually."

"C'mon. I'm hungry. It'll be all right. At least we know Marc."

As unobtrusively as possible, Neil and Jon pulled out the two chairs closest to the end of the table, sat down across from each other and emptied the contents of their lunch bags. Instantly, all conversation at the table ceased. For the next twenty minutes the only sounds that came from the table occupants were open-mouthed chewing and belching.

"Maybe tomorrow we should put up a 'No faggot losers allowed' sign," said Thorne, rising from his seat when the bell for fifth period rang, as he pulled a comb from the back pocket of his Lee Jeans to run through his already perfectly coiffed, feathered blonde hair.

"I really *hate* that guy," said Neil, when Thorne led his clique from the table and out of earshot. "And what's up with Marc? He pretended we weren't even here."

"Well, we didn't say anything to him either," answered Jon.

26

"Yeah, but Marc knows we don't know any of those Woodbridge guys. He could have said *something*. It's like he's embarrassed to be my brother."

~~~

"Where's the fire?" Marc asked Neil three hours later, as the brothers changed for practice in the locker room. "Practice doesn't start for fifteen minutes."

Still upset at his brother, Neil didn't answer and hurriedly laced up his sneakers.

The first player on the court, Neil grabbed a ball off the floor and pounded dribbles into the hardwood, as he made his way to the nearest hoop. Way too pumped up, Neil missed long on his first ten shots. His heart racing, Neil chased down the rebound on the last miss and stepped to the free throw line to regain his composure.

Unlike other players, who could effectively channel their anger into helping them play better, Neil had never been able to perform well when mad. Good free throw shooting, he knew, demanded intense concentration; there was no place for anger at the charity stripe. Taking three dribbles, he bent his knees slightly and eyed the rim, cradled the ball on his fingertips, aimed for just over the front rim, flicked his right wrist and watched the ball arc toward the hoop. Neil knew it was going in as soon as he released it. Now, the only question was whether it'd be a swish or touch any part of the rim. He hoped it would be the former, because to Neil, there was no better sound in basketball. Following the flight of the ball toward the center of the hoop and over the front rim, Neil heard the net pop with a swish. The ball dropped softly under the hoop and took two vertical bounces, as if commanded to do so. Neil couldn't have asked for a better placement of the ball than if he'd climbed a ladder and gently dropped it through the basket.

The teen retrieved the ball and in seconds was shooting and swishing it again. After a few more makes he was completely relaxed, thinking positively and his mind, body and spirit were all working in harmony. Jogging, deep-breathing exercises, or listening to classical music, had nothing on the benefits to be had from perfectly executed free throw shooting.

~~~

"Guys, we're going to change things up a bit today and tomorrow," said Coach Preece, standing in the middle of the circle of kneeling and sitting players before the start of practice. "Because there's so many of you we want to make sure everyone has an equal shot to show us your skills before the first cuts on Friday. So, after our regular drills, we'll break up into teams and scrimmage on the main court. While that's going on, the rest of you will shoot around on the side hoops and wait to be called for one-on-one sessions with Coach Krotzen."

To Neil's relief, the shooting touch he found the day before and had in his pre-practice free throw shooting was still with him in the warm-up drills. And to his surprise, his defense and ball handling picked up. *Maybe I just needed a couple days to work the rust off,* Neil thought, as he huddled with the other players after the last drill ended.

"In the first scrimmage, let's have Harrell, Todd, Hutcheson, Parillo and Dante versus Jessup, Thorne, Martin, Harper and Bricker," said Preece, reading off his clipboard the names of those who'd be playing in the opening game.

Immediately taking charge, Thorne gave his teammates their on-court assignments.

"Shadow, you take Todd; Jess, you got number twenty three; Marty, you take number six; I'll take Hutch and... what's your name, man?" asked Thorne, pointing at Neil.

"Neil Bricker."

"You got Harrell. Okay, Bricker and I will be the guards. Jess, you're in the middle and Marty and Shadow, you guys are the forwards. Let's go."

Neil's team controlled the tip. Thorne demanded the ball and began running the offense, motioning his teammates around the court. Thorne hadn't communicated to Neil in the huddle which guard spots the two were to assume, but now it was apparent that Thorne would be the point guard. By default, Neil took the shooting guard spot. Within three dribbles, Thorne spotted Marc momentarily free under the hoop. From twenty feet, the Woodbridge youth whistled a pass between two defenders that Marc caught and promptly laid in off the backboard for the game's first basket.

Now on defense, Neil picked up his man as he dribbled along the right sideline. Matching him step for step, Neil didn't see a kid from the other team lining him up to be picked. Switching to his left hand, the dribbler led the unsuspecting Neil directly into the path of the screener. Running into the larger boy's chest, Neil was stood up straight and then toppled backwards onto the floor, looking up through the cobwebs in his head just in time to see his man drive to the basket for an uncontested lay-up.

"Stay with your guy!" Thorne screamed at Neil, taking the inbounds pass and dribbling past his still prone teammate.

Scraping himself off the court, Neil jogged unevenly towards the frontcourt trying to regain his senses and balance, while running the index finger of his right hand over his braces-covered front teeth to make sure they were all still in his mouth. They were.

Shortly after passing half court, Thorne threw up an errant long-range bomb that was rebounded and quickly taken the other way. Backpedaling on defense, this time Neil had his head on a swivel looking for picks. Hoping to entice the ball handler Thorne was guarding to throw a lazy pass in his direction, Neil intentionally gave his man a five-foot cushion. The strategy worked and the dribbler telegraphed a pass that Neil intercepted.

Dribbling unguarded along the left sideline, he spotted Thorne in full sprint a few feet ahead of him in the middle of the court shouting for the ball. Neil passed it to Thorne and now the two were racing side by side with only one defender between them – a classic fast break. Soon, the defender would be forced to commit to guarding one of them – most likely, the ball handler, Thorne. Neil anticipated a return pass that he could take in for an easy lay-up. It never came. Instead, Thorne ignored the wide-open Neil and took his defender one on one, tossing up a tough, contested shot that somehow dropped in the hoop.

"That's not how to do it," Neil mumbled to himself, running back up the court.

Relying on his speed and quickness, Neil continually shook loose from his man when his team had the ball. Yet, except for the one steal, he couldn't get his hands on the ball. Thorne hogged it and would either call his own number on offense or pass the ball to one of his friends, who'd shoot it. Neil felt invisible, as if his team was playing four against five. After about ten trips up and down the court without receiving a pass, it was obvious to Neil that Thorne was freezing him out. There could be no other explanation, a seething Neil reasoned, for why a *shooting guard*, of all positions, who was always getting open, wasn't involved in the offense.

Standing behind Thorne in the hallway with the rest of the players during the five-minute halftime, waiting to take a drink at the water fountain, Neil couldn't contain his anger any longer. But sounding more like Charlie Brown than Charles Bronson, any hope Neil had of coolly pulling the confrontation off disappeared as soon as he opened his mouth.

"I'm on the team, too, you know," said Neil, in a voice that rose two octaves higher than usual and quivered with emotion.

"Say what?" asked Thorne, wiping water from his chin with the front of his t-shirt.

"I'm...I'm open nearly all the time and you...you haven't passed me the ball once," Neil stammered.

"Play some defense and you'll get the ball."

"There's nothing wrong with my defense. I got a steal that you gotta basket off of, remember? The only time my guy scored was when...was when I was picked – and that wasn't even my fault. Someone shoulda yelled that a screen was coming."

"You wanna do something about it, faggott? Loser?" sneered Thorne, taking a step towards Neil, as the eight other players from the two teams circled the pair.

31

Neil backed away and lowered his gaze from Thorne's steely blue eyes.

"I didn't think so," Thorne hissed, after about five seconds of awkward silence that to Neil seemed like five days.

"Jerk-off," mumbled Neil under his breath, in a low voice meant only for his own ears to hear, after Thorne had spun around.

"What's that?!" demanded Thorne, wheeling about to face Neil again before executing a two-handed chest pass to the face of rock star Peter Frampton emblazoned across the front of Neil's t-shirt. The force of the shove sent the scrawny boy into a row of lockers, then onto the floor. Lying on his back, Neil's head pounded with pain, but what was left of his dignity was bruised even worse when Thorne stood over him and pointed a menacing finger.

"I'll pass to whoever I want to – faggott *Prick*er!" laughed Thorne, before walking back into the gym with some of the other players.

"You okay, Neil?" asked Marc, taking a knee by his fallen brother.

"Never better. How's it look?" answered Neil, gingerly touching the back of his head for evidence of blood, then leaning forward so Marc could check for damages.

"You'll live. That was a dumb move, you know. He could've really hurt you."

"Why do you care?" asked Neil, rising slowly to his feet.

"What's your problem?" asked Marc. "I'm just trying to help."

"Thanks for nothing. You'd better get back before Thorne and your Woodbridge buddies see you. I wouldn't want to ruin your reputation."

"Have it your way, man."

CHAPTER 4

Alone in the hallway, Neil briefly considered cutting his losses and quitting tryouts on the spot. But after a few deep breaths, the shaky-legged freshman walked back into the gym just as halftime was ending and took his place on the court with the rest of his teammates.

Yet, while Neil was there in body, his mind was still in the hallway on that dirty linoleum floor. Starting the half on defense, a distracted Neil quickly lost track of the player he was guarding and got scored upon, incurring another vicious tongue lashing from Thorne.

"I thought you said there was nothing wrong with your D," shouted Thorne.

Jogging back up the court, a grim-faced Neil knew he wouldn't be involved in the offense in this half either. If Thorne hadn't passed to him before their hallway skirmish, there was no way Neil would be getting the ball now. Neil practically ensured this prophecy would come true by giving Thorne as wide a berth as possible – practically running away from him whenever his antagonist had the ball.

For the rest of the scrimmage, Neil acted like he was playing dodge ball rather than basketball. Trudging off the court at game's end, Neil climbed the bleachers to the top row and took a seat by himself far away from the other players. Lost in his thoughts and self-pity for the rest of the practice, Neil never heard Coach Krotzen yell his number out calling him to report to a side court for his one-on-one session.

~~~

"How many points did you score in your scrimmage?" Jon asked Neil on the walk home after practice.

"Zip," answered Neil solemnly.

"Take many shots?"

"Zero."

"Really?"

"Can't shoot when you never touch the ball. Thorne ran the point and only passed to the kids he knows. Right, Marc?"

"He'd have thrown his arm out trying to reach you, you were so far away from him," answered his brother. "You made it easy for him not to pass to you."

"I could have been standing next to him and he wouldn't have thrown the ball to me," replied Neil.

"Did you say anything to him about it?" asked Jon.

"Yeah, in the hallway at halftime," answered Neil.

"How'd he take it?" inquired Jon.

"He pushed me into some lockers," replied Neil. "Then he called me 'Pricker.'"

"Pricker?! Hey, that's the closest he's come to knowing your real name," said Jon, with a laugh. "We were 'faggot losers' at lunch."

"He called me that a couple times, too," said Neil.

"Thorne's not too big on synonyms, is he?" said Jon.

"Maybe because he thinks you *are* gay," interjected Marc, with a shrug of his shoulders.

"Come again? We?!" asked a confused Jon. "He thinks Neil and I are gay?! Why?"

"Probably because you sit together by yourselves at lunch every day," replied Marc.

"Wait a minute…how does that make us gay?" posed a befuddled Jon.

"I dunno, but Thorne and some others were joking about you being two kinda wimpy-looking dudes, who never talk to chicks and only seem to hang around each other," explained Marc.

"Why didn't you tell them we're not gay?" demanded Neil.

"Like I said, it was a joke," said Marc. "Don't worry about it."

"I hope you're right," moaned Jon. "I'd rather go back to being anonymous than be tagged with that reputation. Hey, maybe Thorne will change his mind about you after your fight, Brick."

"Some fight," huffed his friend, winding up his right leg and booting a rock laying in his path down the sidewalk. "I was on the ground for longer than I was standing up. I don't want to talk about this anymore. How'd your scrimmage go?"

"Not bad. I scored six points on three of five shooting, grabbed three rebounds and had two steals," answered Jon, who, like Neil, had an actuary-like recall for sports statistics.

"Did you guys have your one on ones?" asked Jon.

"Nope," said Marc.

"Me, either," replied Neil.

The following day, with Thorne not even playing in the same game, let alone on the same team as him, Neil performed better in his scrimmage – making both of his shot attempts on long-range jumpers.

"Guys, bring it in," yelled Coach Preece, after he'd blown his whistle to signal the close of practice. "Good work again today, fellas. As you know, tomorrow's the first cut-down day. Coach Krotzen and I have some tough decisions to make, but regardless of whether you make the cut or not, we want to thank all of you for trying out.

"Okay…the names of the boys who've made it to the last round of cuts will be posted on my door tomorrow at noon. We'll see those players again at practice. For those who don't make the list, I encourage you to keep working on your games and give it another try next year for the jayvee team."

~~~

"Do you want to check the list now or after lunch?" Jon asked Neil the next day, haphazardly tossing an armful of books into his locker, before fishing out his lunch bag.

"Let's do it now," answered Neil, talking into his adjoining locker. "I'm curious about who didn't make it. Then we can eat."

Neil and Jon made their way through the maze of corridors, now swollen with four grades worth of students on their way to the lunchroom, to the coaches' offices on the other side of school. Arriving at Preece's door, the boys found about twenty of their classmates and competitors already there, all jockeying for position for a better view of the cut-down list.

Anxiously waiting to learn their basketball fate, the two friends lined up behind the others and watched the chaotic scene – a mixed bag of emotions, with alternating voices of joy and disappointment – unfold.

Gradually, those ahead of Neil and Jon began to peel away from the door and the two wormed their way forward. Taking a cursory glance, Neil noticed the names – almost illegibly scrawled in long hand – were not in alphabetical order. Starting at the top of the page, he began to read down the list.

"There I am!" exclaimed Jon, pointing to his last name written in the middle of the yellow-lined notepaper.

Reading slowly and concentrating intently, so as not to miss his name, Neil continued to scan the list. He passed Jon's name and proceeded down the page. Neil wasn't especially nervous before, but now his heart beat faster and faster with each passing name that wasn't his. After about the first fifteen names he knew there were only a few left. He read on. Hutcheson. Harper. Drapo. And then the list ended. Thinking maybe he'd somehow overlooked his name, Neil started over from the top, this time carefully running his index finger over each name. Hutcheson. Harper. Drapo. *Again*, he reviewed the list. Neil's heart and head pounded in rapid synch and his eyes began to lose their focus from the intensity of his staring. But three times wasn't the charm. He wasn't on the list for first cuts.

For a moment, Neil couldn't move. He looked at Jon in shock and tried to speak, but could only choke out an unintelligible gasp.

"Let's go," said Jon sympathetically, curbing his own excitement and motioning with his head towards the cafeteria.

Settling into a table for two, Neil got only as far as removing the baloney sandwich from his lunch bag. Picking it up and eating it seemed like too much effort. The way he felt – hands shaking and stomach churning – even taking in nourishment intravenously required more strength than he could muster.

All around Neil, playing in stereo, was the usual lunchroom chatter. He'd heard it five days a week for the past two and a half months, but because he'd always been talking with Jon, had never really listened to it until now. On this day, it seemed louder, like a giant, concussive wall of sound that threatened to detonate his head.

"I just don't get it," Neil finally said, after several minutes of silence, looking at his friend through glazed eyes. "I knew it would be tough to make the team, but I thought I played a little better lately and would *at least* make it past the first cut. Did you see some of the names on that list? Horton?! Wagner?! C'mon. I'm better than those guys."

"I know," said Jon understandingly. "There's no way they can make the cut and you don't. You've been playing fine the past couple days. And you did alright in your one on one, right?"

"I didn't have mine."

"Really? Everyone was supposed to have one."

"Think they just forgot about me?"

"Could be. If they did, then you gotta good gripe. I'd tell the coaches."

"Yeah, that *has* to be why I got cut. What else could it be? Hey, I'm glad you at least made it to the next round."

"I think you will, too, once you talk to Preece. When are you gonna say something?"

"Right after school," mumbled Neil through a mouthful of Wonder Bread, the revelation having suddenly restored his appetite, as well as his spirit.

~~~

When the last-period bell rang, Neil reacted like a sprinter breaking out of the block at the sound of a starter's pistol, and made a beeline to Coach Preece's office. Knocking on the half-opened door, Neil found the coach seated at his desk, talking on the phone. Seeing Neil at the door, Preece raised the right index finger of his free hand, indicating that he'd only be on the phone a moment longer.

Neil retreated to the hallway to wait for the coach to finish his call. As the minutes ticked slowly by, though, and Preece's intermittent laugher spilled out of the room, it was apparent that the coach was in no hurry to end his conversation. All Neil could do was lean against the brick wall, painted in the school's red and white colors, and obsessively check his Star Wars wristwatch every minute. Finally, after almost fifteen minutes had passed, Neil heard the phone nestle in its cradle.

"Coach, can I talk to you for a minute?" asked Neil, appearing under the doorframe.

"Not now, son," said Preece, who was already out of his chair and about to brush past the youth. "Sorry, that call took longer than I thought. Can it wait for another time?"

"But, coach, I wanted to…," stammered Neil meekly, calling out to Preece, who by now was halfway down the corridor.

Rationalizing that his argument for another tryout would certainly be lost if he followed and pestered the coach, Neil let Preece go. Heading home, Neil decided that before practice the next morning – hopefully, when the coach wasn't so rushed – would be a better time to plead his case.

"You didn't make the team, huh?" said Al, knowingly, when he saw his son walk through the back door of their house thirty minutes later.

"Well, I'm not sure yet," replied the boy, who then filled his father in on why he thought he'd been cut from the team.

"That makes sense. But why didn't you remind the coaches yesterday?"

"I forgot about the one on ones."

"But every other kid had one, right? How could you have forgotten?"

"I don't know. I just did."

"Well, you're already a practice behind after today, so I wouldn't wait any longer, if I were you. You should try to talk to him tomorrow. And if you can catch him well before practice starts he won't feel pressed for time and might be more receptive."

"Good idea."

"Marc made the first cuts, I'm guessing."

"Yeah, his name was on the list."

~~~

Early the next morning, Neil beat Jon to their school-walk meeting spot. Dressed for practice, just in case, Neil waited five anxious minutes before he finally saw his friend about one hundred yards away, rounding the corner and slowly jogging toward him along the tree-lined street.

"Where've you been?" asked Neil, when Jon came within earshot. "I can't be late."

"Sorry, I couldn't find my sneakers. Hey, this is a switch. Five days out of the week you're late and *now* you're on time?"

"That's because this is important."

"Where's Marc?"

"Still getting ready, I guess. C'mon, let's go."

Neil and Jon arrived at the high school twenty minutes before the scheduled start of practice – plenty of time for Neil to seek out and engage the coach in conversation.

"Good luck," said Jon, veering off into the locker room. "See you on the court."

Neil continued walking down the athletic wing until he got to Preece's office. The door was closed and no one answered his knock. Waiting for the coach to show, Neil rehearsed in his head the speech he'd carefully scripted the night before. *Coach, I was cut and I think it's because I didn't have my one on one like everyone else. Could I have my test today and then you can decide if I can go on to the final cuts?*

Neil assumed his case was convincing enough, now all he needed was an audience with the coach to prove it – assuming Preece ever arrived. By now, though, it was five minutes to 8:00, with still no sign of the elusive coach. Neil's hopes for having a one on one about his one on one were fast slipping away. To make matters worse, the other freshmen basketball hopefuls were filing past him on their way to the gym; Neil hoped to conduct his tête-à-tête with Preece in private. Now, if it happened, there'd be spectators.

CHAPTER 5

"You haven't left this spot since yesterday, Pricker?" laughed
Thorne, spotting Neil as he exited the locker room and walked
toward him on his way to the gym. "Think your name will
suddenly appear on the list or something? Let's see…nope, sorry,
Pricker. Not there. You're still *cut*."

Neil didn't respond; he didn't know how to, which was just as
well. After the pushing incident, the last thing Neil wanted was to
give Thorne a reason to hit him.

"Really, what are you doing here, Pricker?" Thorne demanded.

"I wanna talk to the coach," said Neil, choking out a barely
audible reply.

"About what?"

"Tryouts."

"Give it up, man. You might not even be good enough to play
on the girls' team."

Laughter arose from some of the players, who'd gathered in the
corridor.

Thorne moved to within inches of the intimidated youth. It was
Neil's move. And although he hadn't been in a fistfight since age
seven, Neil knew enough to suspect that Thorne was waiting for an
excuse to take his abuse to the next level. Neil weighed the pros
and cons of striking his adversary; the immediate gratification he'd
feel about wiping the smug smile off Thorne's face, versus the pain

that would almost certainly be visited upon him once his rival retaliated.

The more Thorne smirked, the more Neil worked to convince himself to suspend his good judgment and pop the punk in the face. It might even be worth the inevitable beat down, just to get one good shot in; to release all his tension against this arrogant and privileged jerk, who seemed to coast through life.

"What's going on over there?" came an adult's voice from down the hall.

"Nothing, coach," said Thorne, turning to respond to Krotzen, who was heading for the crowd huddled outside of Preece's office.

"Don't you have someplace to be, Mr. Thorne? All of you should be in the gym warming up. Go! I'll be there in a minute."

"Coach?" asked Neil, a moment later when the crowd dispersed. "Is Coach Preece here?"

"No, not today," said Krotzen, inserting a key in his boss' office door. "He's attending to a personal family situation."

"Well, can I ask you something?"

"Later. I'm already running late for practice."

"Okay, but, technically, I can't practice. I got cut yesterday. That's what I wanted to talk to you about. You see…"

"Well, you're going to have to talk with Coach Preece. What's your name?"

"Neil Bricker. I never had my one on one and…"

45

"No?"

Pushing the bill of his baseball cap up his high forehead, a visibly annoyed Krotzen licked his index finger and flipped quickly through the pages of his clipboard, before stopping to read the sheet where the one-on-one evaluations were recorded.

Is there any place this guy doesn't *wear a hat?* Neil thought, picturing the coach sporting one while showering or having sexual relations with Mrs. Krotzen.

"Here's why," said Krotzen. "It's because on the day I called you for it, you weren't at practice. You can't skip practice without a good excuse and expect to make the team."

"But, I *was* at every practice," protested Neil. "Guess I didn't hear you call my number."

"Well, I musta repeated it two or three times. If you don't respond, what else am I gonna think, but that you didn't show?"

"But I didn't hear."

"Listen, Coach Preece will be back at practice on Monday. I suggest you talk to him then. It's just me today running the show. I don't have time to give you a one on one."

Without waiting for a response, the coach turned his back on Neil and walked toward the gym.

Exiting the school, Neil was hit by a blast of cold air that momentarily pushed him back inside, as if God was giving him a sign to go back to the gym and talk to Krotzen again – and not wait for a Monday audience with Preece. To politely but firmly ask the man who was in charge of administering the one on ones to give him his fair shake; nothing more, nothing less. But instead, Neil turned his jacket collar to the wind and the hint, left the building and walked home.

"What's the verdict?" asked Al, a half hour later, pausing from raking up leaves on the side lawn of the family's property, when he saw Neil trudging up the sidewalk toward the house.

"The head coach had a family situation, or something, and wasn't there, but I talked with his assistant," replied Neil.

"And...?"

"He said I'd have to talk with Coach Preece on Monday."

Al leaned on his rake and opened his mouth as if to speak.

"What?" asked Neil.

"Nothing," replied his father, picking leaves off the teeth of his rake before setting it back on the ground and resuming his chore. "Never mind."

Neil gave his father a quizzical look and then continued on his way.

"Hey, got any plans this afternoon?" his mother asked from the driveway, as Neil was about to open the back door to the house.

"Not now."

"Rather than watch the boob tube, do you wanna go to Paterson with me?" she continued, stuffing a cardboard box filled with non-perishable food items into the back of the family's 1974 red and white Volkswagen bus. "I could use some protection."

Neil laughed slightly to himself, while ambling over to his mother. He knew very well that even at five-foot-nothing and one hundred pounds, Ann was *more* than capable of handling herself in the inner city of Paterson, New Jersey.

Once a month for the past several years, Ann made mostly solo trips to a soup kitchen in the heart of the city's slum to drop off boxes of donated food. She knew her way around the city better than most residents, so if anyone needed a bodyguard there it was Neil, not Ann.

Raised in a blighted neighborhood in the Park Slope section of Brooklyn, Ann learned early in life how to take care of herself both verbally and physically. Many adversaries – such as teachers, who she felt were too hard on her kids, and fellow Eastham residents, who spoke ill about the family for adopting Marc – felt her wrath or were stung by her icy glares and cold shoulder. Few people messed with Ann Bricker twice.

"Sure, I'll go," Neil said, idly picking with his fingers at the fraying "McGovern-Shriver '72" bumper sticker pasted to the back of the VW. "Who could turn down a trip to beautiful Paterson? Besides, I got nothing better to do."

~~~

Located just ten miles south of Eastham in bordering Passaic County, Paterson once had a reputation as one of the most prodigious silk producers on the eastern seaboard. But by the late 1970s, "Silk City's" days as a major manufacturer seemed as distant as the memory of its last uncorrupt politician.

Following the familiar script of other northern industrial cities, Paterson's businesses and factories either dried up or relocated and its economy spiraled. Race riots ensued and scores of white residents fled to the safer, neighboring suburbs. Left in their wake were poor blacks, too unskilled and undereducated to punch their own one-way ticket out of town.

Paterson's illegal drug trade flourished and its crime rate soared. A quarter of the city's 150,000 residents now lived at, or below, the poverty line. Once a source of state pride, New Jersey's third-largest city was now a first-rate example of urban decay and neglect.

"Remember the last time you were here?" Ann asked, making a right-hand turn on Market Street in downtown Paterson and pointing the VW south along Madison Avenue.

"September, 1976," responded Neil quickly, as if he'd studied the date for a quiz. "I'll never forget it. There was a small rat crawling on a pipe in the kitchen ceiling of the church basement, where we dropped off the food."

"Oh, yeah. That's right. Well, don't worry. I haven't seen a rat down there in I don't know when. Was that why you stopped coming?"

"No, but it didn't help. I dunno…you always seemed to come down here on Saturdays and I usually had a game or a practice for something on those days. Either that or you already had dad or Molly along for the ride. Has Marc ever come with you?"

"Not yet."

"What's he waiting for? I'd think he'd wanna come back to see his old friends and neighborhood."

"He's said he wants to visit, but like you with your sports conflicts, he's always had something going on on the days when I've gone to the church."

"How many years have you been coming here?"

"Since before you were born…so, probably sixteen, seventeen years now."

"Ever think you'd be doing that this long?"

"Nope. I thought by now a country as wealthy as ours would have figured out a way so its citizens wouldn't go hungry."

"Did Marc and his mom ever go hungry?"

"Oh, yeah. His mother told me sometimes they had so little food that they had to eat maple syrup sandwiches for dinner."

"Maple syrup sandwiches?! He never told me that."

"He was probably too embarrassed. That boy ate like a horse the first summer we hosted him in the "We Care" program. He musta gained ten pounds in two months."

"What made you and dad get involved in We Care, anyway?"

"Ever notice how many black people there are in Eastham?"

"None…except for Marc."

"That's right. Your father and I wanted you, Molly and Gerry to have an appreciation and understanding of another race and culture – one that's maybe not as well off as ours."

"I remember that first summer we hosted him, people in town kept staring at him like he was some sort of space alien."

"He was an alien, in a way. Hosting an inner-city black youth was practically unheard of, but that was small potatoes compared to when Marc's mom died and we adopted him. We learned quickly that trans-racial adoptions just *aren't done* in our community. Everyone knows their neighbor's business in a small town like Eastham – right down to which side of a person's head that they part their hair on. So, you can imagine how curious people were when Marc and *his* hairstyle moved into town."

"So, why'd you do it then?"

"There wasn't much choice. He didn't have any living relatives. The alternative was foster care and we didn't want to see Marc end up there. That would have been a dead end for him. Plus, you were what, twelve, when we took him in permanently? You two were so close then. You shared everything from a bedroom to ball caps. Besides, your father and I figured we'd be doing our part to make sure there'd be three fewer racists in the world; pretty tough to not like black people when your own brother is black."

Ann made a left turn on Beckwith Avenue and pulled the VW bus up to the curb in front of St. Cecilia's Church.

"You know, I think we've covered as many bases as we could to make sure Marc's had as easy a transition as possible," Ann said, turning off the engine, before leaning back against the head rest and gazing out the driver's side window. "It's funny. The first

51

thing we did when we adopted Marc was to have your father bring him down to the police station and introduce him as a member of our family. A subtle way of making sure the town cops wouldn't stop him when they saw him on the streets alone. I think it worked."

Ann and Neil exited the car and brought the first load of boxes up to the church. Impeccably maintained and ornately designed, the church could have been mistaken for any suburban house of worship, were it not for the razor wire fence that surrounded it on three sides. Sandwiched between a bail bonds shop and a liquor store, the stately, turn-of-the-century structure stood out in the neighborhood as absurdly as Neil would at a boy-girl party.

Setting his box down in the basement pantry, Neil couldn't help but steal a wary look at the ceiling, fearful of seeing a rat scurrying across the exposed pipes. Relieved to find it apparently rodent free, but still not completely satisfied that one or more weren't homesteading somewhere else in the room, Neil hustled back outside to continue unloading the car. On his last trip back to the kitchen, Neil found his mother talking to a volunteer from the neighborhood.

"Mrs. Davis, do you remember my oldest son, Neil?" asked Ann.

"Is *this* Neil?" asked the elderly black woman, putting on her glasses that had been dangling from a chain around her neck and breaking into a warm smile. "How old are you now, son?"

"Fourteen, Mrs. Davis," answered Neil, setting his box on the floor. "I'm a freshman in high school."

"A freshman?! My heavens. I remember when you used to come here and you were no taller than a fire hydrant. Now look at you. You've gotten so tall. Next time you come, bring your best friend with you, okay?"

"Jon?"

"No, Marcus. Marcus Harper. You two boys used to be joined at the hip. How is he?"

"He's good, but…ahhh… we're not really that close of friends anymore."

"Friends come and go, but no matter what, you'll always be his brother. Remember that. And in Paterson, brothers have each other's backs – *especially*, when times are tough."

Yeah, sure, Neil thought, while nodding politely. *Just like during basketball tryouts when Marc just watched Thorne push me around.* "Okay. Well, nice to see you again, Mrs. Davis."

Neil excused himself and went outside to wait in the VW for his mother.

"Mom, can we go by Marc's old place on the way home?" asked Neil shortly thereafter, when Ann returned to the bus.

"We could, it's only a few blocks away," said Ann. "Why do you wanna go there?"

"No real reason; just to see what it looks like now."

A few minutes later, Ann turned the VW up Alabama Street and pointed to the Alexander Hamilton Public Housing Project, a

53

charmless high rise so blighted that the Founding Father for which it was named was undoubtedly cringing through eternity at the thought of the "honor."

"There it is, in all its glory," said Ann, easing her foot off the gas pedal, so her son could take in the scene. "Is it like you remember?"

"Yeah," said Neil. "Boy, it doesn't look like *anything's* changed around here. There's garbage everywhere and even the building next door is still a mess. Would've thought it'd been torn down by now."

"It's like Paterson's answer to Rome's ancient ruins – minus the tourism."

"I'll bet the elevators in Marc's building still don't work. Never liked going in there. Whenever we did, people looked at us like they'd never seen white people before."

"Can you blame them? Other than cops and social workers, we may've been the only white people to go in there."

"With good reason. That place was a dump. It gave me the creeps."

"Oh, it wasn't that bad. You only had to go there a few times – always during broad daylight – and nothing bad ever came close to happening."

"Yeah, well, it still felt weird."

"Imagine how it felt for Marc when he moved to Eastham. That had to be weird for him; the only black kid at that school…everyone watching his every move. But you have to give him credit. It wasn't easy for Marc at first, but he worked really hard to adjust to his new environment and now he fits in great. And most importantly, he's happy. Sometimes, I wonder if his friends even notice his skin color. I think they just see Marc, the person, not Marc, the black boy."

Pressing the right foot of her size five Birkenstock sandals down harder on the accelerator, Ann sped the car up again, turned onto Interstate-80 and chuckled.

"What's so funny?" Neil asked.

"Oh, I was just remembering something cute you said once when you were little," his mother replied. "Funny how certain locations trigger certain memories. Whenever I hit this on-ramp, I always think about what you said to me here on our way home one day. You were no more than four or five and you turned to me and said 'Mommy, we're leaving the black world and going back to the white world.' Even then you knew the difference between Paterson and Eastham."

~~~

Twenty minutes later, Ann pulled the VW into the driveway.

"Got any plans before dinner, Neil?" asked Al, who was now raking the small patch of lawn near the back door of the Bricker house.

"No. Why?" asked Neil, suspiciously, as he exited the bus and shut the passenger-side door.

"You do now. Grab a rake from the garage and help me finish bagging these leaves. It's supposed to rain tonight and I wanna get 'em off the ground before they get wet and heavy."

"Aw, why do I always have to rake the lawn?"

"Because we love the others more than you."

With an exaggerated roll of his eyes noting his displeasure, Neil retrieved the spare rake – the one with half its teeth missing – and returned to the rear of the house.

"Rake the side lawn," said Al, tossing Neil a box of rolled up leaf bags.

A half an hour later, a listless Neil had raked a small section of the lawn into a neat pile, when a sudden gust of wind blew in from the east, swirling the leaves like they were in a funnel cloud, before scattering them about.

"Crappy wind," said Neil, re-raking a new pile and then angrily and quickly stuffing the dead foliage into a green plastic bag before another blast of cold air could undo his work again.

Neil had a love/hate relationship with his family's property. There were so many varieties of trees on the Bricker's large lawn, and it seemed to him that they all shed their leaves on different weeks. Consequently, too many autumn weekends, in Neil's view, were wasted raking the lawn. Every fall, Neil's argument to his parents to let all the leaves drop and then rake them up together fell on deaf ears. There were simply too many of them, Al countered. The family would be drowning in a sea of leaves by Thanksgiving. No, it was much more manageable to rake in stages.

Even more frustrating for Neil was that he did the work gratis, as his parents didn't have the disposable income to pay their kids an allowance. "Ya get to live here for free. How's that for an allowance?" said Al, when Neil once asked to be paid for doing his chores.

When not working on the land, though, the list of fun things for Neil and his siblings to do on it stretched as far and wide as the two-acre spread itself. With its folksy, lived-in charm, the property where the Bricker's old farmhouse rested represented a simpler time when lawns were mowed, not manicured, and played on, rather than preserved. Planted in the side of the driveway opposite the house was a basketball hoop with a backboard perched atop a wooden pole. A three-point shot away stood the two-car garage – a converted barn, complete with hay loft, where the kids put on haunted houses to entertain their friends on Halloween. Connected to the back of the garage was an empty boat house. Next to that, stood a brick and mortar well that was once the property's sole source of water, back when the land was a working farm. Now safely boarded up, the kids amused themselves with the old relic by dropping small rocks down the hole in the center of the cover and counting how many seconds it took before the stones kerplunked at the shallow bottom. And running behind the well was a four-foot-high rock wall – still standing as sturdy as when it was first constructed a century ago to keep farm animals from straying onto the back neighbors' plot.

The L-shaped lawn started in front of the house, wound down a gentle pitch, turned left at a proud, five-story oak tree and extended some fifty yards to the back of the property. Pachysandras on the left and a cluster of towering pines to the right encased the side lawn. Where the grass ended, two rows of grape vines began, intersecting the yard and winding about seventy-five feet down the hill into a briar patch of wild raspberries and blackberries. Parallel to that, a fenced-in garden, filled with rows of meticulously planted tomatoes, green beans and corn on the vegetable half and roses, irises and hydrangeas on the flower side. Beyond the orchard stood a majestic American elm and under it a small swath of grass that led up to the western face of the garage.

In temperate weather, Neil and his siblings spent hours a day taking turns swaying like a pendulum from the tire swing that dangled from the tree's meaty limb. And when they tired of that, they played wiffle ball, or hung out in the pop-up camper parked next to the garage, or picked bushels of berries and grapes and sold them at the curb to passing motorists.

On summer nights the kids ran barefoot around the property collecting lightning bugs in Mason jars, while Al and Ann watched in amusement from their wicker rocking chairs on the wrap around front porch sipping from tall, perspiring glasses of iced tea.

To take his mind off raking that Saturday, Neil recalled those fun times spent in the yard. Losing himself in his memories, the subsequent two hours that it took for him to finish raking and bagging the side lawn passed as quickly as if he'd slept through it.

When Neil had hauled the last of the full leaf bags to the curb, he put the rake away in the garage and went into the house. Reaching for the refrigerator door, Neil winced as his fingers gripped the handle. Quickly withdrawing the hand he looked down to see the base of every finger was covered with fresh, bubbling blisters, developed during his afternoon of raking. *Odd*, Neil thought, that he didn't feel the pain before. Apparently, he was so focused on the task at hand, or too distracted by it to notice. Either way, he'd been working hard, that was for sure – the friction of bare skin rubbing against the wooden arm of the rake causing the blisters.

Pressing the index finger of his left hand lightly over each blister, Neil made the serum fluid underneath them move about from side to side and up and down. What was previously a boy's soft, pampered hand, was now nearly unrecognizable to him. His was a hand with history, with character; one that had something to show for its manual labor. Neil squeezed it tightly, making the sensitive-to-the-touch blisters burn even more. He knew his hand would hurt but he didn't care. Neil wanted to feel the pain – the physical evidence of his accomplishment that afternoon. He'd earned it. This was what it felt like to work hard and the pain was his. Unclenching his fist, the sting in his hand began to subside. *Maybe a certain measure of pain and discomfort*, Neil wondered, *was meant to accompany a job well done. Maybe they went together, hand in blistered hand.*

CHAPTER 6

After failing the previous week to talk with Preece and Krotzen, Neil was determined to get face time with at least one of them as soon as possible the following Monday. Rather than wait until the end of the school day, Neil excused himself from fourth period Study Hall to seek one of them out.

Arriving at Preece's closed door, Neil rolled his eyes and wondered if he'd ever catch the coach alone. Knocking anyway, the teen was surprised to hear a voice call out from behind the door.

"Enter."

Opening the door, Neil poked his head in to find Preece sitting cross legged at his desk, folding up the Sports Monday section from *The New York Times*.

"Coach, Preece?" asked Neil, tentatively stepping into the office.

"Yeah, c'mon in," replied Preece, removing his sneaker-clad feet from the desk and sitting up in his chair.

"Do you have a couple minutes to talk?"

"Sure. Sit down. What can I do for you...?"

"Neil...Neil Bricker. I tried out for the freshman basketball team."

"Sorry. There are so many kids at tryouts. What can I do for you, Neil?"

"Well, I was cut last week and I think it was because I didn't have my one on one."

"No? Everyone was supposed to have one."

A puzzled-looking Preece swiveled around in his chair and withdrew a folder from a file cabinet.

"You're right," the coach replied, after finding Neil's name on a sheet in the folder. "You're not listed as having one."

"So, can I get...," started Neil.

"But you're also listed as being absent on Thursday."

"No, I was there."

"Coach Krotzen indicated in the notes that he called for you, but when you didn't answer he assumed that you dropped out of the tryouts."

"But I didn't drop out. I really was there."

Preece closed the folder, raked a lock of chestnut-colored hair on the left side of his head that extended to his ear lobe with his fingers and searched for the right words to say.

"Well, here's the thing, Neil. We don't really have any comments on your sheet – good or bad," Preece said sympathetically. "There's a couple notes about your ball handling, but that's it. You didn't really stand out to us and now, a few days have passed. We've moved on in the tryouts. Maybe if you'd let us know immediately about this oversight, we could've... I'm sorry, son."

Neil's face grew flushed as he tried to hold himself together.

"You don't remember me from the shooting drills?" he asked in desperation, in a cracking voice that betrayed the composure he was slowly losing his grip on. "I was really good at those."

"No, I don't remember. And evidently, neither did Coach Krotzen. Again, I'm sorry. You're welcome to try out for the jayvee team next year, though."

With that, Preece rose from his chair, signaling that the conversation was over.

Neil averted the coach's eyes, for fear that Preece would see the tears welling up in them and backed slowly out the door, fisted hands clutching his metaphorical walking papers.

In the empty hallway, Neil's legs felt unsteady and weak, as if he'd taken his first steps after being bed-ridden for a week with the flu. Despite all his worrying about not making the team, he still wasn't psychologically prepared for the reality of it.

Wanting to be alone, Neil ducked into the nearest boy's restroom, headed for a stall, closed the door behind him and sat on the toilet lid. With arms folded over his lap, Neil forlornly stared at the tile floor. Replaying his conversation with the coach as if it was on a continuous loop, Neil kept getting stuck like a needle on a scratched record on one of the coach's sentences: *"You didn't really stand out to us. You didn't really stand out to us."*

For a kid whose self-esteem and identity were so tightly tethered to his athletic ability, no other words could hurt more. Slowly, quietly, Neil released his built-up tears. It had been years since he last wept and his muffled, halting sobs sounded like forced hiccups. But the more he cried, the more natural it became and soon Neil couldn't keep his raw emotions at bay; the dike behind his face broke, unleashing wave upon wave of tears that streamed in crisscrossing ribbons down his cheeks.

Neil cried not only because he was cut, but for the person he was and the person he'd never be. *Who else*, he thought, *would bawl like a baby over something as stupid as not making a team? I bet none of the other kids who got cut cried about it on a toilet seat. Marc wouldn't have cried if he'd been cut. No way would Thorne have either. They were cooler than that.*

How come being on a team – even if I was only the last man at the end of the bench – is so important to me?

The answer came to Neil the way it usually did in his moments of introspection and word association – channeled from a song by his favorite rock music group, the Who. In this case it was the lyric "Got a feeling inside (can't explain)," from "Can't Explain."

Perhaps Thorne was right about him, Neil thought. Maybe Neil was a loser. Winners don't run away from the ball because they're afraid to butt heads with someone. They're competitors, who aren't thrown by adversity, but plow through it.

Sitting on a toilet seat, head in his hands, weeping, the difference between a winner and a loser came into stark focus for Neil. The bill had finally come due on a lifetime of timid passivity and the cost was pain like none that had ever visited him.

~~~

Suddenly, the fifth-period bell crashed Neil's self-pity party. With the change of classes, he knew that surely someone was about to invade his privacy. Wiping tears from his face, Neil took a few deep breaths, swallowed hard and tried to collect himself. Leaning over to his ankles, he looked below the stall's walls to his left and right to find that no one else was in the restroom. Emerging from the stall, Neil went to the row of sinks and looked in a mirror to assess the damages. As he suspected, staring back at him were puffy, red-rimmed eyes. Anyone who came into the restroom now, Neil knew, would immediately know that he'd been crying. Mockery and maybe even physical punishment would be in store for him should the wrong upperclassman or ninth grader walk in and see him in his present condition.

Turning on the faucet to full blast, Neil sunk his cupped hands in the hard spray and soaked his face. Blotting it dry with a paper towel, Neil took a hesitant look back in the mirror. *Better*, he thought. Taking a few more deep breaths, Neil burst out of the restroom, head down, and darted and weaved like Pac Man, through the packed corridors to the other side of the school – careful not to make eye contact with anyone.

"Hey, I was just about to go to lunch without you, where were you?" asked a miffed Jon, leaning against his locker, when he saw Neil round the corner of the hallway.

"I talked with Preece last period," answered Neil, in a low, cracking voice. "I'm officially cut. He said I didn't make any real impression in the tryouts, so giving me my one on one now wouldn't make any difference."

"Bummer."

"Listen, I don't really feel like being here right now. I'm gonna go home."

"But you can't cut class. You'll get in trouble."

"Then, just make something up for me, will you?"

"Okay. We got Gym, History and English left. I'll tell the teachers you threw up at lunch and went home sick."

Neil reached into his locker, grabbed his jacket, slipped out a side door and made his way home. All he wanted to do was shut himself in his room and circle the wagons around his pain. With his father at work and siblings and mother in school, Neil knew he'd have the house to himself for a few hours.

The long walk home gave Neil ample time to feed his discontent about life at East Hill; seeds that were planted fifteen years earlier when Eastham – in an enrollment-generating move intended to curb the flight of students to a newly constructed parochial school in the county – scholastically merged its high school with the more affluent village of Woodbridge.

Almost overnight, the transfusion of students and money converted a failing, skeleton of a school into an athletic and academic powerhouse, with an array of college-prep classes, taught by some of the most handsomely compensated teachers in the state.

Woodbridge parents weren't content just to have their children graduate from East Hill; that was a given. For them, it was never a question of which college or university their children would attend, but which *Ivy League* school they'd write their tuition checks to.

But the upgrade came at a steep price that not even the wealthy Woodbridge parents could afford to pay. East Hill earned a reputation as a teenage wasteland, where many students coped with

65

the intense pressure to succeed by regularly abusing drugs and alcohol.

Woodbridge and Eastham's marriage of convenience highlighted the vast socio-economic differences between the two northeastern New Jersey communities. Many Woodbridge teens seemed to enroll at East Hill with an air of self-importance and sense of entitlement – never missing an opportunity to boast how they descended from CEOs and CFOs, while reminding their Eastham peers that they were merely the sons and daughters of CPAs and C-O-Ps.

The same youths often bragged about expecting to receive their own new Corvette or Mercedes the day they earned their driver's license. Neil, meanwhile, figured he'd be lucky to borrow his dad's decidedly un-cool AMC Pacer – assuming it lasted that long.

While money was always tight on his father's teacher's salary, Neil didn't know what he was missing out on until he overheard his new classmates nonchalantly talk about their sprawling homes – complete with in-ground swimming pools and tennis courts – and exotic trips to resorts on remote islands that seemed as far away and inaccessible to him as Mars. The only "vacations" he usually had were a night or two at his cousins' duplex in Union City, New Jersey – a place no one who'd visited would *ever* confuse with a tropical paradise.

Suddenly acutely aware that he was "poor," Neil would pull his baseball cap down over his eyes and sink into the back seat, like a suspect trying to conceal his identity while being taken into police custody, every time his mother in her four-wheeled heap dropped him off at school on a rainy day. The self-conscious teen never prayed harder than when asking God to keep the battered, old VW bus with a grapefruit-sized hole in its muffler from stalling out on school grounds, further prolonging his embarrassment.

~~~

By the time Neil got home, his grief had morphed into anger. Needing an outlet for his hostility, he ran upstairs to his bedroom and delivered two punches to his pillow. Scanning the room for a more satisfying inanimate victim to hit, Neil's eyes landed on his old, used, six-piece Ludwig drum kit tucked into a corner. That would do.

Fumbling through his and Marc's stacks of tapes, Neil searched for something with an edge to play along to. Tunes with teeth sharp enough to cut through his adolescent angst.

The Eagles. No. Neil wasn't in a "take it easy" kind of mood. Chicago. No. "ABBA?!" Neil exclaimed, tossing Molly's audiotape of the Swedish pop group over his right shoulder while wondering how it got into the pile. "*Shit*, no!"

Finally, Neil came across his copy of *Who's Next*, by the Who. Neil had worshipped the English rock and roll band ever since the seventh grade when he'd seen *Tommy* on late night TV, the film based on the group's rock opera album by the same name.

Raised a Roman Catholic, Neil had been Baptized, received his First Holy Communion and been Confirmed, but the closest he'd ever come to a religious experience was when he listened to *Tommy* for the first time. Songs like "Sparks," "Pinball Wizard," and "We're Not Gonna Take It," with their powerful, yet poignantly arranged music and lyrics, brought him closer to a divine spirit than any bible passage he'd read, prayer he'd recited or homily he'd heard. It was all Neil could do not to drop to one knee, make the sign of the cross to his Gods – The Who's Pete

67

Townshend, Roger Daltrey, John Entwistle and Keith Moon – and say "amen" every time he heard that album.

The band occupied such a large quadrant on Neil's limited sphere of reference that he was surprised to once read an article in *The New York Times* that had "WHO" and "drugs" in its headline only to find that it referred to the World Health Organization and not his favorite band.

Like his parents' generation, who could recall where they were the day Buddy Holly was killed in a plane crash, Neil's seminal moment when the music died for him occurred the year before in eighth grade English class, when word spread amongst his classmates that Moon, the Who's legendary, manic drummer, had died of an apparent drug overdose.

Unable to afford drum lessons, Neil was self-taught and it showed. He was an inconsistent time keeper on his snare and hi-hat cymbal and rarely pulled off seamless fills around the kit. Neil learned how to drum by mimicking along to songs he heard on the radio, audiocassettes, and by watching rock bands play on late-night syndicated broadcasts of *Don Kirshner's Rock Concert*.

Who's Next, with two of his favorite songs that emphasized furious fills on his snare drum, mounted and floor tom-toms, heavy strikes to crash cymbals and a minimum of tame, polite time keeping, was exactly what Neil had been searching for that afternoon. Neil popped the cassette into his tape player, pressed rewind, plugged in a pair of headphones and settled onto his drum stool. Waiting for the tape to reverse, he impatiently twirled his drumsticks in his hands and got himself mentally ready to play. When the tape stopped, Neil pressed play and cranked the knob on the volume up to eight. Despite the initial blast of sound being louder than Neil expected from the iconic synthesizer opening in the first track, "Baba O'Reilly," he didn't turn the music down. The Who wasn't meant to be experienced at ABBA volume level. When the extended, computerized keyboard ended, Neil simultaneously hit both of his crash cymbals hard in synch with the music before launching into his first fill.

Out here in the fields
I fought for my meals
I get my back into my living
I don't need to fight
To prove I'm right
I don't need to be forgiven
Yeah, yeah, yeah, yeah, yeah, yeah

The lyrics, sung by lead singer, Daltrey, struck a raw nerve with Neil as he continued his animal assault on the drum kit – playing whatever the song called for, only with more aggression and attitude than he'd ever shown before. The tune required dozens of hits on his cymbals, which Neil unleashed with visceral ferocity, imagining with each strike of his sticks that he was bringing them down against Thorne's head. Alone in his room, it was as close as the inhibited boy dared come to strike out in anger against a bully, but it still felt real and satisfying. And with each ensuing hit, the power and torque behind his arm swings became stronger and stronger.

At song's end, an already perspiring Neil looked at his sticks – or what was left of them. Five minutes earlier, they'd been practically new and almost unmarked. Now, an inch from the one in his left hand was shorn off and the plastic tip of the one in his right was missing. Neil's focus had been so intense, that he hadn't noticed he'd been playing too hard or had apparently been an equal opportunity drummer: banging out a beat on the drums' metal rims as often as on its skins.

Nonchalantly tossing the broken sticks in the air to an imaginary audience, as he'd seen Moon do in vintage concert footage, Neil reached down to the sleeve attached to the side of his snare, retrieved two more sticks and fast forwarded the tape past "Bargain," "Love Ain't for Keeping," "My Wife," "The Song is Over," "Getting in Tune," "Going Mobile" and "Behind Blue Eyes." All great songs, but somewhat lacking in the extended intense drumming he was in the mood to play along to. Stopping the tape in time for the last track, "Won't Get Fooled Again," Neil pressed play. At eight-and-a-half minutes long, the song was Neil's favorite and on this particular day – and in his current, agitated state of mind – the title had a personal significance to him. Neil childishly promised himself he wouldn't get fooled again either – even though he wasn't sure about what.

Guitarist, Townshend, christened the song with a pull on a power chord, leading into yet another lengthy synthesizer break, that to the impatient Neil seemed to last as long as last-period English class. Finally, the drums were called in and Neil responded by slamming his crash cymbals once, then concurrently pounded out beats on his floor tom and snare multiple times. Proceeding to beat the crap out of his kit – yet still in total synch with the music on the tape – it was difficult now for Neil to tell his playing from Moon's. When Daltrey's voice broke in, Neil seamlessly switched to keeping time and mixing in fills.

We'll be fighting in the streets
With our children at our feet
And the morals that they worship will be gone
And the men who spurred us on
Sit in judgment of all wrong
They decide and the shotgun sings the song

70

I'll tip my hat to the new constitution
Take a bow for the new revolution
Smile and grin at the change all around
Pick up my guitar and play
Just like yesterday
Then I'll get on my knees and pray
We don't get fooled again

Neil played the rest of the song with a consistent searing vengeance. He wasn't technically sound, but for that matter, neither was Moon. And Neil wasn't nearly as quick with his hands as the late drummer was, so he didn't strike every beat on his fills all the time. But every drum or cymbal he did connect with was pounded on with a purpose.

For the next two-and-a-half hours, Neil played these same bookend *Who's Next* songs over and over on nothing more than anger, adrenaline and a can of RC cola. Finally, after channeling all his hate and frustration into his playing, fatigue won out. With nothing more to give, Neil switched off the cassette recorder and removed his sweat-soaked headphones. Neil had been playing for so long that as he took them off, he could almost hear the music linger in suspension for a split second before being sucked away into a vacuum. In his now silent room, the only thing Neil could hear was the ringing in his ears, the consequence of having played the music loud and long.

Slumped on a stool, his "Keep on Truckin'" t-shirt soaked through to the front and back and worn corduroys sticking to his perspiring thighs, Neil looked at his sticks. They were somehow still intact, but badly dented and chipped from the many times they'd missed their mark and hit the rims. When he did manage to make contact with the skins, he hit them so hard that they were filled with more pockmarks than an acne-scarred adult's face.

71

CHAPTER 7

"How was school today?" said Neil's mother, knocking on his door while entering the bedroom.

Neil looked away and didn't reply.

"Neil, what's wrong?" asked Ann, coming closer, her eyes squinting with concern.

"I talked to the coach today," answered Neil, swallowing hard and still unable to look his mother in the eyes. "Tried to see if he'd let me have my one on one…"

"Right."

"He said I hadn't really shown much during the tryouts and…"

"You were cut?"

Unable to bring himself to say the words, Neil bobbed his head in the affirmative.

"Oh, kiddo," said his mother, wrapping her arms around the boy's shoulders. "I'm so sorry."

"Ann? Neil? You up there?" yelled Al from the bottom of the attic steps.

"C'mon up, we're talking," Ann shouted to her husband.

"What's going on?" asked Al, after he entered the room.

"Neil got cut from the team today," said Ann.

72

"You talked to the coach, Neil?" Al asked.

"Yeah…didn't do any good, though," answered Neil, breaking loose from his mother's embrace.

"Well, I wouldn't have waited three days to speak with him," blurted out his father, finally voicing his pent-up annoyance over his son's lack of assertiveness. "I would've camped outside his office the *first* day you found out you weren't on that list. You'd have shown him how much you wanted it and it wouldn't have given him time to forget you."

"*Al*, the last thing he needs now is for 'I told you so's' or hindsight," shot back Ann, incredulous over her husband's lack of sensitivity.

"That's not the reason, I got cut," added Neil. "He said I didn't make enough of an impression in the scrimmages and drills."

"Well, it couldn't have hurt…" said his father.

"Al, *enough*," interrupted Ann curtly. "No need to beat him down any more."

"You know, Neil," said Ann, "maybe with an extra year of practice and another growth spurt, you could make the jayvee next year."

"Doubtful," remarked Neil bitterly. "I'm done with basketball – at least at that school. I really hate it there. I've been thinking, can I transfer to St. Rita's next semester."

"Why? Have you suddenly found religion?" responded Al sarcastically. "It's not because you didn't make the basketball team, is it? If so, that's not a good enough reason. Either way, it's a moot point. We can't afford St. Rita's tuition right now."

"There's too many snobby, rich kids at East Hill," replied Neil. "I don't fit in there."

"So, there's *no one* from Woodbridge you like?" asked Al.

"Not really," mumbled Neil, talking into his chest.

"And you don't think there'd be jackasses at St. Rita's, too – and *rich* jackasses, at that?" continued Al, his deep voice rising in agitation. "I've got news for you: Just because it's a religious school – a Catholic school – doesn't mean every kid who goes there is a good person. You probably couldn't throw a bible there without hitting a bad apple. Neil, there are jerks in every level of society and in every religion. Everywhere you turn you'll find 'em. Jesus Christ, they make up half the damn population!"

"Do you have a problem with someone in particular at school?" Ann asked her son in a soothing voice.

"Sort of," downplayed her son. "Some kid at the tryouts pushed me into some lockers once."

"Who is it?" asked Ann, her tone doing a one-hundred-eighty-degree turn from understanding and nurturing to defensive and confrontational. "The principal should know about this; that boy's *parents* should know this is going on, too!"

"You don't know him. He's from Woodbridge. And *don't* call the school! The *last* thing I need is for the principal to get involved."

"I'm not surprised it was a kid from that town," snorted Ann. "They learn that behavior from their parents. Whenever I ring doorbells there to collect for "We Care," I'm consistently turned away. I had one woman say to me, 'We Care?! We could care *less*!' and then shut the door in my face. Million dollar homes and they can't afford to help out the less fortunate...they should be ashamed of themselves. Strange people, too. I went into some houses where there was hardly any furniture. It's like they spent all their money on these status-symbol houses and then had nothing left to furnish them."

"Good God, Annie, you carry a grudge like Pavarotti carries a tune," sighed Al, interrupting his wife's rant with one of his own. "Let's not paint them all with the same brush, okay? I'm sure not *every* Woodbridge resident is like that. But Neil, running away and transferring schools won't solve anything. You have to learn to deal with bullies now because you're going to run into them in every phase of your life, whether it's a kid at school, a coach or a boss. People don't change – particularly, bullies. They just adapt to more subtle, socially acceptable ways to push people around – away from hitting to hurting others emotionally and psychologically. My point is, Neil, either stand up to a bully or ignore him. It's your choice, but you can't let them get to you."

"Can we not talk about this anymore?" Neil asked, growing tired of the lecture and now rising from his drum stool.

"Sure, honey," said Ann, patting her son on his damp shoulder. "We'll call you when dinner's ready. Between now and then, maybe you should think about taking a shower."

When his parents left the room, Neil pulled himself up on his bunk bed and flopped on the mattress. Rolling over onto his stomach, Neil caught sight of the basketball drills manual on his desk. The one his father had given him and Marc. Jumping off his bunk, Neil moved the little white box that held his unused silver bracelet to one side and flipped through the booklet. Suddenly, Neil's eyes were drawn to a headline that read: "How to tell a winner from a loser." Skimming the page, he came to the last paragraph and began reading to himself: *You can't wish to be good. You must work at it during the off-season. Even when you don't necessarily want to, you have to work. It's the only answer.*

It was everything his father told him months ago, boiled down to four simple sentences. A reminder of what Neil knew on the first day of practice, when he was eliminated from a ball-handling drill – but had later fooled himself into thinking that his superior shooting ability would overcome. Neil could be angry at Thorne, Krotzen and the school all he wanted, but in his moment of clarity and introspection, it was now apparent that he alone was to blame for not making the team. The coaches were right. He didn't have enough good moments during the tryouts and it was all because he hadn't worked hard enough to improve in the summer and fall.

A week later, Jon and Marc found out they made the basketball squad – albeit just barely. Judging by who did and who didn't make the final cut, Jon calculated that he was probably the twelfth man on the twelve-man roster, with Marc being the eleventh man. Knowing that Jon was a better player than he somewhat eased Neil's mind, but was still small consolation given the circumstances of how he got cut.

His best friend otherwise preoccupied with basketball in the afternoons and on weekends – and no sports activities to keep himself busy – Neil now found himself with too much spare time on his hands. Normally, his sure-fire cure for the fall and winter blahs was to lose himself shooting baskets in the driveway. But Neil had lost much of his enthusiasm for the game and could barely bring himself to touch a basketball, only reluctantly rebounding for Gerry when his brother wanted to shoot baskets on the driveway hoop.

Neil drifted aimlessly in the following weeks, showing little interest in anything. Like the ongoing energy crisis that gripped the nation, Neil was listless and run down. Not even drumming seemed fun to him anymore in the wake of the early December tragedy at the Who's concert in Cincinnati that left eleven fans dead and scores more injured. His life took on a dull, predictable routine: School, playing Atari video games in the afternoon, dinner and TV, with homework only squeezed in during the commercials that ran between *Barney Miller*, *B.J. and the Bear*, *The Dukes of Hazzard*, or the dozen other primetime sitcoms he tuned into each week.

Marc and Jon's first game in early December offered Neil a break – be it unwelcomed – from his tedious schedule. His emotional wounds still exposed, it was all Neil could do to feign school spirit for a team that had no use for him and which included Thorne in its starting five.

"That's nice you came to support your brother and sister," said Ann to Neil, as the Bricker family settled into their seats on the East Hill wooden bleachers shortly before tip-off. "Marc and Molly both said they were excited to have you come."

"Uh- huh," mumbled Neil, seriously doubting that his brother and cheerleader sister had expressed anything close to that sentiment.

With Thorne leading the way, East Hill dominated the game from the start and held a commanding halftime lead over visiting Pascack Valley High School. Picking up where he left off, Thorne continued his hot shooting in the second half – almost single handedly outscoring the opposition.

Having to sit through Thorne's offensive explosion was about as much fun for Neil as attending Sunday Mass, but seeing the cocky youth get away with showing up his opponent and yelling at teammates turned Neil's stomach. Having read *A Clockwork Orange* the previous summer, Neil felt as though he was reliving the part where a character was coerced into watching violent, disturbing images against his will. *Jesus Christ*, Neil said to himself, *the only thing missing to complete this nightmare is the headgear to force my eyes to stay open.*

As if what was happening on the court wasn't tough enough for Neil to take, equally as nauseating to him was the scene in the stands. Throughout the game a man sitting below the Brickers made a spectacle of himself, obnoxiously and loudly cheering on the home team and abrasively challenging every official's call that went against it.

"That guy's a real treat, isn't he?" grunted Al during a timeout, with a look of displeasure. "Seems to be number one on our side's father. Look, now he's coaching his son from the stands, when the kid should be listening to his coach. I don't care how talented that kid is, if I was a betting man, I'd say he quits the game before his senior year. See the way he looks at his father? You can see it on his face. That boy doesn't want to be here. He *hates* playing right now. I don't care how many points he's scored."

"Do you know who number one is, Neil?" asked Ann, when her husband finished his monologue and play had resumed. "He's very good."

"His name's Bobby Thorne," answered Neil. "He's from Woodbridge."

"He's also a very good ball hog, is what he is," said Al, resuming his harangue. "The coach needs to sit his butt down. Maybe that'd teach him and his old man that basketball's a team game."

"Which is the boy you had the problem with, Neil?" asked Ann.

"He didn't make the team, either," Neil said, eyes fixed on Thorne, hoping his lie would end any future discussion involving the bully.

"Good," huffed Ann. "I don't like to see people rewarded for poor behavior."

"Right," answered Neil, watching Thorne exit the game to a chorus of cheers from the crowd.

"Well, we're up by twenty with two minutes left," recapped Al. "Hopefully, Marc will make a cameo in the game soon."

Seconds later, at the next dead-ball whistle, both Marc and Jon popped off the East Hill bench, peeled off their warm ups and checked into the game.

It was prime garbage time, but with Thorne out of the game and his best friend and brother now playing, for Neil it was the most compelling part of the contest.

Rusty from nearly a game's worth of inactivity, Marc and Jon struggled to get into the rhythm of the action during their first few trips up and down the court. Marc, by far the less skilled of the two, was particularly slow to get into the flow, committing a turnover on a travel call the first time he touched the ball.

"Ahhh," sighed Al, before coaching out loud to no one in particular. "He's rushin' himself. Marc's nearly a head taller than anybody else out there. All he's gotta do is take his time. No one can stop him if he does that...except for himself, of course."

Six feet five inches tall, with arms that stretched below his knees, at first impression Marc looked every bit the part of a stereotypically great basketball player – until he stepped on a court. In elementary school and high school, these physical characteristics – plus his inner city upbringing in Paterson – led teammates and coaches alike to believe that Marc *must* have game. But with two left feet and the equivalent of two left feet for hands, first impressions quickly gave way to the reality that Marc had no game whatsoever. Still, he had one of the most important traits for long-term basketball success: Height, and any coach who crossed his path figured that with great length as a baseline, physical maturity and coaching could develop Marc into a quality player. Currently, however, any potential he had was locked inside his gangly body.

Al buried his head in his hands and shook it in disbelief, as Marc got the ball again on the next possession and proceeded to toss up an air ball from point-blank range.

With less than five seconds to go in the game, Jon touched the ball for the first time, inbounding the ball near Pascack Valley's basket. Taking the return pass, he dribbled twice to his right, set his feet and from about twenty-five feet away – roughly the distance of the NBA's new three-point line – launched a high-arching arrow just ahead of the final buzzer. The crowd let out a collective gasp at the long – and seemingly forced – shot, but Neil knew better than to be surprised. Jon was more comfortable taking a bomb like this than he was a lay-up.

"That's going in," Neil said softly, as he watched the spinning ball's descent, an instant before the rest of the fans erupted in applause to the perfect swish of the net – now folded over the left side of the rim.

"How'd you know that?" Ann turned to him and asked, a curious smile breaking across her face.

"That's about the only type of shot he takes when we play," Neil said with a shrug.

After filing out of the gym with the rest of the crowd, the Brickers sat in their idling VW bus in the school parking lot, waiting to give Molly and Marc a lift home.

"What were Marc's teammates calling him?" asked Ann, twisting her body from the passenger seat of the front row to face Neil. "I couldn't make it out."

"Shadow," answered Neil.

"Shadow?! What's that about?"

"It's his nickname. It's from *Saturday Night Live,* when Bill Russell, the old Boston Celtic, guest starred and was the coach to a team of white players. They called him the 'Black Shadow.'"

"I don't get it," said a puzzled Ann.

81

"It's a takeoff on the *White Shadow* TV show," explained Al. "The coach is white and his players are black."

"Well, it seems to me like they're making fun of Marc," replied Ann.

"It's just teenagers being teenagers," said her husband. "They could call him far worse, you know. So long as Marc doesn't mind..."

Far worse, Neil said to himself, *would be "faggott,"* the nickname he was tagged with during basketball tryouts.

~~~

One game was all it took to convince Neil that he had to find a way to avoid attending future contests. Neil found it when he landed a part-time job as a referee in Eastham's fifth and sixth grade boys recreational basketball league – arranging his work schedule so that he was reffing games in conflict with those weekday nights and weekend afternoons when the freshman team played.

"You really earned your bread today, Neil," came a voice from behind, as Neil bent over to take a drink from the water fountain in the Eastham Elementary school hallway, after working a game in late January. "That guy in the stands was on your back big time."

Turning around, Neil recognized Dave Cavenall, a sophomore at East Hill and a teammate of his the previous summer on Eastham's fifteen-year-old-and-under travel baseball team.

"Oh, hey, Dave," said Neil. "Not like I'm really able to keep track while I'm doing a game, but your brother looked like he played pretty well today."

"He was, when you weren't calling him for bogus fouls."

"Up yours," Neil said with a laugh.

"Just kidding. Hey, baseball tryouts are coming up in a few weeks. You going out for the freshman team?"

"I plan on it."

"Trying out for center field?"

"Yeah. Why?"

"You'll have some competition. I hear Bobby Thorne played center at Woodbridge last year. He's supposed to be really good."

The words struck Neil like a bean ball thrown between his eyes. While Neil suspected that a great athlete like Thorne probably played baseball, too, he hadn't considered the possibility that his basketball antagonist might also play the same position as him. Hearing Dave's news made Neil's muscles recoil and his stomach drop to his Pumas.

"You shouldn't have much to worry about," offered Dave, sensing he'd upset the freshman. "You're a good player. Although, Thorne is Krotzen's pet."

"Uhhh…what does Krotzen have to do with anything?" asked Neil hesitantly. "Isn't Preece coaching freshman baseball?"

"From what I hear, Preece is coaching jayvee and Krotzen the freshman team."

Neil hadn't been expecting this curveball. He'd assumed that Krotzen would be Preece's assistant again – as he was for football and basketball. Even though Preece had cut him from the basketball team, Krotzen was the coach who Neil disliked – the latter man's brusque, macho attitude and suspected prejudice against non-football players being the main reasons. Neil didn't want to – or even think he *could* – play for a coach like Krotzen.

Dave and Neil talked for a few more minutes, but what about, Neil would have been hard pressed to recall, he was so distracted by this bombshell. All he could think about was how Thorne and Krotzen would now be huge obstacles to his making the baseball team.

Snapping out of his daydream, Neil was suddenly aware of his surroundings. Rec league players and their families now jammed the hallway and all of them seemed to be talking at once. Feeling claustrophobic and suffocated, Neil abruptly ended the conversation with Dave, grabbed his heavy winter jacket and headed for the exit. It was past 7:00 p.m. and in the twilight, the already frigid day felt even chillier. But still feeling hot and flushed from having refereed the game, being in the congested hallway and hearing Dave's news, Neil welcomed the biting cold, leaving his navy blue parka unzipped.

Neil crossed the small, wooden footbridge built over a rock-filled stream that led from the school to its outdoor sports complex and walked through the middle of the triangular-shaped field. Three baseball diamonds were at each point, with a soccer field bisecting it – its goals still planted in the ground some two months after the season ended.

Neil wasted no time worrying about what awaited him in six weeks when baseball tryouts would begin. Soon, the two center fielders from adjoining towns would be competing head on for one starting spot on their high school's freshman baseball team.

And with Krotzen as the coach Neil knew that the deck was clearly stacked against him. Krotzen would surely favor Thorne, the star athlete he'd coached for two consecutive sports.

The last couple months had been the worst and emptiest of Neil's life. Not a day had gone by that he didn't regret his failure to prepare for basketball tryouts. Cutting across the deserted, wind-swept field, a lucid moment poked through Neil's doubts and fears. Neil realized that he couldn't afford to just show up cold for baseball tryouts, with the same passive approach he took to basketball practice, and expect to perform well. He couldn't leave anything to chance – not with Krotzen for a coach. His chance meeting with Dave Cavenall was the cue he needed. If Neil wanted to avoid that post-basketball-tryout letdown in the future, then the only way to overcome it was to arrive at tryouts on day one, hitting and throwing like it was July, instead of March. He had to start working out for baseball season *now*.

Motivated by his fear of failure rather than paralyzed by it, Neil broke out into a light jog around the perimeter of the soccer field. After completing two laps he walked to a stop and bent over at the waist. Looking up, Neil saw the steam from his wet breath framed against the glow of the moon looming over the far goal. Then he was off again, this time sprinting across the field, grunting with every stride through teeth gritted so tightly Neil could probably press license plates in his mouth, if he had to. The soles of his old sneakers offered little traction on the frozen turf and his flapping, heavy winter coat forced him to work harder against the stiff breeze blowing in his face. Neil felt like he was running with an open parachute attached to his back, but he kept going, arbitrarily setting a goal to run ten straight sprints on the one hundred yard field before he'd allow himself to quit.

But ill outfitted for the task and improperly warmed up, Neil completed just six dashes before falling to the ground on all fours. Sucking hard for air, he gagged and felt the familiar queasy feeling that often overcame him as a child, when getting sick to his stomach from binging on candy seemed like a weekly occurrence. Neil's throat tightened and before he had a chance to repress the reflex, vomited the undigested Reggie bar – named after New York Yankees' slugger Reggie Jackson – that he'd wolfed down after the basketball game, onto the frozen turf.

"Maybe this wasn't such a good idea," Neil wheezed, spitting out the remains, then wiping his mouth off with his jacket sleeve.

His sides cramping as if clamped in a vice, Neil rolled onto his back to try and relieve the pressure in his stomach. Still fighting to catch his breath, he stared up at the black sky, his mind racing with ideas about what type of physical fitness routine to undertake that would get him in the best possible baseball shape. Neil remembered a recent article in *The Sporting News* about a Chicago Cubs player whose off-season workout regimen included plunging his arms into a gunnysack of rice and rotating his hands to strengthen his wrists and forearms. *That'd work*, he thought. *What else can I do? C'mon, think.*

Baseball was Neil's first love; the first sport his father taught him and as he improved at it, Neil began to associate baseball with good times and good food. If he played a particularly impressive game, his parents treated the family to takeout pizza for dinner. Long after the meal ended and everyone else had left the dinner table, Neil would linger there, still in full uniform, nursing a soda – his victory cigar – and drink in the moment for all it was worth. On nights like that he delayed showering for as long as possible for fear of washing off the bliss and accomplishment of his stellar game and risk reverting back into a pumpkin, a nothing. After his basketball failure, baseball was all Neil had left now. Lying on the frozen soccer field, a nauseous Neil hungered to experience that pizza dinner afterglow again.

~~~

When he got home that night, Neil ran straight to his room to record his baseball workout ideas before he forgot any of them. With Thorne otherwise preoccupied with basketball, Neil planned to use the next six weeks to get a leg up on his rival – regardless of whether Thorne had any idea that the two would soon be competing for the same position on the team. Whether it was drumming, lifting weights, working his arms in a sack of rice, swinging a weighted bat, hitting off a tee, throwing, or running sprints, Neil vowed that not a single day would be wasted between now and the start of practice.

"Dad, can I show you something?" asked Neil, standing in the entrance of the parlor, clutching a sheet of paper, moments after preparing his workout-routine schedule.

"What's this? Homework?" asked Al, setting aside his issue of *Life* and reaching for the list.

"Nah, something more important," Neil responded, taking a seat on the bench that ran underneath the parlor windows directly behind Al's old La-Z-Boy recliner. "It's some stuff I thought I could do to get ready for the baseball season."

Adjusting the reading glasses perched on the end of his nose, Al read the paper silently to himself, occasionally nodding his approval.

"You think I'm missing anything?" Neil asked impatiently.

Al didn't speak and continued reading.

"The running and hitting go without saying," said his father, a few seconds later. "Drumming, huh? Four days a week?! How come that many?"

"I read somewhere that a major leaguer learned how to drum and it improved his wrist and hand speed and gave him better bat control," answered Neil.

"I always thought your swapping my old golf clubs for that drum kit was the worst trade since the Indians gave up Manhattan Island for beads and trinkets," Al half joked. "Now, I'm convinced of it…yeah, sure, you can play. So long as it's during reasonable hours – and I've got earmuffs.

"I like the rice idea. Where'd that come from?"

"An article in *The Sporting News.*"

"Well, that helps justify the yearly subscription rate. I'd lose the bench press, though. If you get too muscular and tight through the upper arms and shoulders it'd hamper your hitting and throwing. I'd substitute wrist curls and handgrips that work the forearms – anything that develops and strengthens those areas, because hands, forearms and wrists are what you use to hit with. Ted Williams and Hank Aaron were two of the best hitters ever, but they weren't big guys. They were fast and strong from their elbows to their fingers."

"That's a pretty ambitious plan," Al continued, handing the sheet back to his son.

"Thanks, dad," said a relieved Neil. "I was thinking about using the boathouse to work out in. Could you help me clean it up tomorrow?"

"You bet. So, what brought this about?"

"Well, I know now that I took basketball for granted and got cut because I didn't work at it enough. I don't want to make the same mistake with baseball."

"Good. Too bad that had to happen, but sometimes the best lessons learned come at a steep price."

With his father's help, the next day Neil converted the empty boathouse attached to the barn into a workout room, stocking it with exercise equipment. In one corner, they set up the bare bones – and barely touched – weight set Neil received as a birthday present years earlier. On the far end was the hitting station. There, they placed a weighted bat and the batting tee Al taught Neil how to hit on. A few feet away, the two nailed an old drop cloth, left over from when the family painted the house the previous summer, to either side of the boathouse's side walls, to absorb the balls Neil would hit off the tee and toss to strengthen his throwing arm. And behind the net, instead of sacks of rice, Neil improvised, using a garbage bag filled with hard sand he'd scooped up from the beach at Crownwood Lake Park in town.

~~~

A month into his regimen, Neil had become addicted to his baseball-workout process. He'd begin jonesing for his drug toward the end of the school day, fidgeting and clock watching his way through last-period English.

When he finally got home, Neil would run twenty minutes worth of sprints on the side lawn and then retire to the cold, dark boathouse for another fix – the only light coming from the late afternoon sun that poured in through the dust-streaked windows. While many of his classmates were slipping behind their respective garages to smoke dope, Neil ducked in back of his to get high on the sense of accomplishment he felt when he taxed his muscles, honed his hand-eye coordination and pushed himself to his physical limits.

But no matter how hard he worked, Neil refused to be pleased with his efforts, believing satisfaction only fed into contentment, which is what got him into trouble before and during basketball tryouts. There was always room for improvement, he convinced himself. He could always do more.

One afternoon Neil realized how far he could push himself, if he had to. While hitting off the tee, Neil lost focus and started daydreaming about how many fingernails Pete Townshend must have shorn off over the years while executing his signature windmill move on the guitar.

"Stop screwing around!" Neil yelled out, when he realized that he'd lost track of how many balls he'd hit. "Concentrate."

Dialing up his intensity, Neil resumed hitting. Starting again from the beginning, he counted out loud as he hit, watching the net swallow each ball. The madder Neil got, the harder and faster he swung and yet the more focused he was on the task at hand. What normally took Neil twenty-five minutes to do, he finished in fifteen. When he hit his two hundredth ball, Neil dropped his bat to the ground, stretched out his cramped fingers and noticed that the palms of each hand were shredded and bloody.

"That was a mistake," said Neil, as the damp winter air stung his raw wounds.

But looking closer at his throbbing hands, Neil saw something else and quickly reached a different conclusion. After all, if Pete Townshend was willing to sacrifice a fingernail or two every once in awhile for the sake of rock 'n roll, then Neil should expect to give a little blood and skin for the sake of his passion. Maybe that's what true commitment to a cause was all about.

CHAPTER 8

For two weeks in late February, the mother of all inspirational sports stories – the U.S. Olympic Men's Hockey team – was splashed across Neil's family's TV set. In moments of self-doubt about his baseball future, Neil need look no further for motivation than the "Miracle on Ice" team of rag tag college kids, who strung together upset after upset on their way to winning the gold medal.

Neil milked the inspirational story for all its worth, wallpapering his bedroom with every press clipping on the team that he could get his hands on. By the end of the Winter Games in Lake Placid, New York, he knew the names and bios of every member of the twenty–man squad. If pressed, he could have probably picked seldom-used reserves like Mark Wells and John Harrington out of a police lineup.

Neil's excitement for the team had reached a fever pitch by the Friday they were scheduled to face the heavily favored Soviet Union team – the same crew that only a couple weeks earlier had crushed the U.S. squad in an exhibition game.

The game was played in the afternoon, but would be broadcast on tape delay in prime time. Neil did the nearly impossible for most of the day – avoiding the radio and TV – so as not to risk hearing the final score.

"Hey, what time should I come over to watch?" asked Neil, calling Jon from the mounted telephone on the kitchen wall two hours before game time.

"You can't," answered Jon glumly.

"Why not?"

"I got invited to a party in Woodbridge tonight. I pretty much have to go."

"You're going to miss the biggest Olympic game ever because of a stupid party?! Geeze, it seems like there's a party there every weekend."

"Yeah, they just rotate it from house to house, depending on whose folks are out of town that weekend."

"Whose party is it?"

"It's at Thorne's house. The whole team's gonna be there. This was the first one I've been invited to. I can't not go to it."

"That must be the same party Marc's getting ready to go to. He can't even stay home on his birthday."

"Oh, that's right. Your folks throw him a party?"

"He's fifteen, not six. We had a cake at dinner and he opened presents. That was it. You have a game tomorrow morning, right? Why would there be a party the night before?"

"I dunno… it's Friday? Some of those guys on the team don't care if there's a game the next day or not. I bet Thorne's probably been hung over or stoned for every Saturday morning game this season."

"This really sucks."

"Well, at least *you* can still watch the game. I don't even know if I'll be able to see it at the party."

"You gonna drink beer there?"

"Not unless they have *root* beer."

"What're you gonna do then?"

"Munch chips, walk around, see if I can find a TV to watch the game on, I guess. Hey, I gotta change clothes and shave. I'm getting picked up in a half hour."

"Shave?! You got like *one* whisker on your chin!"

"It's still one more than you have. Hey, I gotta look good in case I get lucky."

"Give me a break. You have to actually *talk* to a girl first before you can get lucky with one. Just in case, don't do anything I wouldn't do."

"You wouldn't do *anything*."

~~~

After refereeing a pair of basketball games the following morning, Neil stopped by Jon's house on his way home to get a recap of his friend's game that day and the party the night before.

"How was the bash?" asked Neil, when Jon greeted him at the front door.

"Not so loud," said Jon, peering anxiously over his shoulder to see if anyone inside his house overheard Neil's question. Turning back to his friend, Jon continued speaking in hushed tones. "My folks don't know I was at a party. I told them I was going over to your house to watch the game. Let's talk outside."

Jon grabbed a basketball from the ball bin in the garage and the two boys began to shoot baskets in the driveway.

"I was gonna call you later," said Jon, still talking in a low voice.

"You missed a great game last night," said Neil, firing a one-handed fall-away jumper that swished through the hoop.

"I saw it...watched it on the TV in Thorne's bedroom."

"What were you doing in there?"

"It was about the only place I could go where kids weren't doing drugs."

"You're kidding."

"I wish. And Marc was doing the most of any of 'em."

"I can't believe that."

"You didn't see him when he came home last night?"

"Yeah, I did. The jerk woke me up. He came in our room and turned the light on. He was bouncing off the walls. He wanted to play the drums, but I told him to knock it off, or he'd wake the whole house up. Then he kept trying to talk to me. He wouldn't stop. I was so tired; I was half listening; but I was awake enough to know that he didn't smell like pot."

"He wouldn't have smelled like pot. He was doing cocaine."

"What?! Are you sure? I mean, I figured he wasn't drinking soda at these parties and probably smoked some pot, but..."

"Yeah, I wouldn't of believed it either, if I didn't see it for myself. Some of his friends were saying he had to try it because it was his birthday."

"Some present. All I got him was a Knicks hat. Why would he do that? That's nuts."

"Who knows, but maybe we shouldn't be all that surprised. He's really changed since he began hanging around with those Woodbridge kids."

"I know. In like a week he went from sitting at our table to eating with the cool kids and sitting with them at football games. He's one of them now."

"Are you gonna tell your folks about this?"

"What would I say? 'Mom, dad, Jon saw Marc doing cocaine at a party.' He'd be grounded until he was thirty, if they didn't kill him first."

"Yeah, that's *exactly* what you should say. Or tell him you heard a rumor about him doing it and say to knock it off or you'll tell your folks. He won't like it, but maybe it'd wake him up. Better him to be mad at you than to end up a burnout druggie."

"That'd be our longest conversation in months."

Neil took a pass from Jon, cocked his arm to shoot the ball and then paused.

"It's sort of funny, you know," Neil said, now following through with his shot attempt.

"What is?" asked Jon.

"My mom told me they adopted Marc to give him a better life, but maybe the only thing they really did was give him a nicer place to get high in.

"Where would kids our age even get that stuff from? Isn't coke supposed to be expensive?"

"They can afford it. You know all those kids have big bucks," answered Jon dismissively. "Maybe one of the juniors or seniors who were there brought it. There were a lot of upper classmen there."

"You didn't drink, did you?" asked Neil.

"I had about three sips of a beer…tasted like piss. I walked around with it for awhile, then dumped it in a house plant."

"Oh, that was really cool."

"Hey, I made sure no one was looking when I did it."

"Was Thorne mad you were in his bedroom?"

"No. He actually told me I could watch the game in his room. He watched it with me for awhile, too, which was sorta creepy."

"Why's that?"

"At school the guy either acts like I don't exist, or he makes fun of me, and now he wants to be alone with me, while there's a party going on in his house? It was just weird. I didn't know what to say to him. Finally, he just got up and left."

"Nice house?"

"It was more than nice. It was something else. He's got a sauna, an indoor pool and a tennis court in the back yard."

"Indoor pool?! Nice life. What time did you get home?"

"About 11:30."

"That must have been an interesting car ride."

"I walked home. The party was still going on when I left and there's no way I was gonna wait around just to get in a car again with Mitch Weller, or anyone else at that party. People were wasted all over the place."

"You walked home from Woodbridge?! That's like three miles away."

"Well, walked and ran. What choice did I have? I couldn't call my dad for a ride and ask him to pick me up there."

"How'd the game go today?"

"We got slaughtered. Lost by twenty. Thorne played like crap. Guess he was in rough shape from last night. Preece benched him the whole fourth quarter."

"How'd Marc do?"

"Worse. He committed a couple turnovers and missed an easy lay-up. I caught him sleeping a couple times while we were on the bench, too.

"But I got to play a lot; got my season high, too: Seven points! You know, if Thorne got wasted the night before every game, then maybe I could work my way into the starting lineup."

As February passed into March, the weather in the northeast took a welcome turn towards spring. The air temperature shot up to an unseasonably high sixty degrees, leaving clusters of puddles and snow and ice patches for Neil to sidestep when he performed his daily sprints on the side lawn.

With baseball tryouts looming, the timing couldn't have been better, even though Neil had experienced enough north Jersey winters to know that he likely hadn't seen the last of the season. On the first Monday of the month, Neil was hacking away at the batting tee when his father stopped by the boathouse.

"So, what's your average against the net?" Al asked from the open door, as sun streamed into the shed.

"Ha. Don't know, but at least I haven't struck out yet," answered Neil, resting his aluminum bat on his shoulder.

"Think you're ready for practice?"

"I guess, but I'd feel more confident if I was able to hit off live pitching and practice fielding."

"True, but it's not like we live in Florida. I'm sure you've still done more preparation than anyone else has. Say, on the way home today I swung by the big diamond at the elementary school. The infield looked too wet to hit on, but assuming you can still catch, you could probably shag flies without getting the balls muddy."

"But that's assuming you can still hit fungos, dad."

"We'll see. Wanna go?"

"Yeah. I'll be behind schedule, though, so just give me a second to get my handgrips, so I can squeeze them in the car."

"Oh, great. I can never hear that grating squeak enough. I don't know if it's helping you or not, but it's made me appreciate your drum playing more."

"Really? You think my drumming's getting better?"

"I didn't say that. It's more like the lesser of two evils."

Al grabbed the bucket of balls and his son's bat and Bobby Murcer Rawlings baseball glove with the New York Yankees outfielder's facsimile signature etched in the oil-stained pocket, while Neil went into the house to retrieve his handgrips. Stepping into his cleats, Neil walked back outside and climbed into the passenger side in the front seat of the VW bus. In a few minutes, the two were at the deserted, soggy baseball diamond, Al standing at home plate and Neil stationed in center field, some two hundred and fifty feet away.

"Back up," shouted Al, the bat in his right hand and a baseball in his left. "I had my Wheaties this morning, I'm feeling strong today."

Neil retreated a few steps and bent over at the waist, resting his closed gloved hand on the top of his left knee and his bare hand on his right thigh, his body balanced and ready to move in any direction.

Al lobbed the ball in front of him, transferred his left hand below his right on the bat handle and took a full swing. He connected, but the ball – having barely struck the barrel of the bat – trickled harmlessly into a puddle to the left of second base.

"Should I back up a little more?" Neil yelled into his father sarcastically.

Al ignored his son's wisecrack, reached into the bucket for another ball and tried again, with only slightly better results – hitting a line drive that took two wet hops before Neil picked it up.

A few more batted balls found puddles, before Al found his rhythm, honed over many years of hitting Neil and the team's he coached, hundreds of balls. Once he got back into the swing of it, muscle memory took over and Al effortlessly lofted towering fly balls to his son.

On the receiving end, the six-month layoff from the last time Neil had shagged flies might as well have been six innings. To him, the skill was like riding a bike. Once Neil learned how to catch them, he knew he'd never forget how. Neil had shagged so many fly balls over the years that at fourteen years old he rarely misjudged a play anymore. Now, he had a seemingly innate ability to determine which angle to take on a line drive or whether to break in or back on a fly ball.

Yet, while he was a good enough center fielder to hotdog it on occasion and catch a ball with one hand, Neil never did. His father taught him the fundamentally correct method – to always use two hands – and implied that no matter how cool he might look using just one, the short-term reward wasn't worth the risk. If Neil caught ninety-nine balls out of one hundred with one hand, he could count on Al reminding him that the lone drop wouldn't have occurred had his son tried to catch the ball the proper way.

Neil tried every defensive position when he learned the game: pitcher, catcher, shortstop, but he gravitated to the outfield, where he felt most at home. As comfortable as how his fingers fit into his broken-in mitt.

The infield, he thought, was too Type A and intense, with too many hard-hit ground balls and screaming line drives. The outfield, though, had a different pace altogether. It was slower and more relaxed. Most of the action there involved fielding high, easy fly balls that seemed to hang in the air for as long as it took him to lope underneath them, before they'd drop from the sky and nestle softly in his glove. To Neil, there was nothing competitive, harmful or remotely angry about a fly ball or pop out. They were the most benignly hit balls in baseball.

Today, roaming the wet outfield, Neil's mind was awash in pleasant memories. When he was first learning the game, practicing at the field with his father was as much of a weekend ritual as yard work and Sunday Mass. Nearly every Saturday and Sunday from March to August, the two would head to the sports complex after dinner – when the day's Little League games had ended and they were assured of getting a field to themselves. With Al hitting his son grounders and pop flies and pitching him batting practice, the two would practice until dusk reluctantly forced them off the field.

In the last year or so, though, as Al's growing family consumed more and more of his spare time, their private sessions at the field grew less frequent. Neil understood. He wasn't resentful. He knew that at nearly fifteen years old, the clock was ticking on how many more years – or maybe even months – that he and his father would be able to share this special time together. So Neil didn't care that the ball field looked more like a Vietnamese rice patty, or that he had to run the balls in to Al after he'd caught four or five in a row, rather than throw and risk getting them wet; anything to keep playing, stay happily stuck in childhood and keep adulthood at bay. Neil would have played in a moat.

"Last one," yelled Al, after about forty minutes of hitting fungos. "Your mother's gonna be expecting us home for dinner soon."

Tossing a ball up before him, a tiring Al swung and hit a soft, low line drive to straightaway center field. Neil broke quickly towards the infield and after about a dozen steps reached down and caught the ball at shoe-top level in the webbing of his glove. Without breaking stride, he ran towards home plate and dropped the ball in the bucket.

"Nice catch. Your prize is you get to carry the bucket to the car," said Al, a bib-shaped ring of sweat darkening the neck of his red duo fold shirt.

"Should I carry you, too, dad? Or can you make it there yourself?"

"Get in the car, wise guy."

Sliding into the VW, Neil held the bucket of balls on his lap – his surrogate air bag and the only "protection" available to him in case of a car accident, with the safety belts of the old bus tucked under the seats, having never seen the light of day.

"Wonder what's been happening in the world since we last left it?" asked news junky Al, turning over the engine, before switching on the car radio to his favorite station, WINS.

"Ahhh, a commercial," snapped Al, shutting the knob off in disgust. "So, tell me again when practice starts?"

"A week from this Saturday," answered Neil.

"That's right. Nervous?"

"Not yet."

"I don't think you have anything to worry about."

"I hope you're right."

"Of course I'm right. I can tell the difference. You're definitely stronger. Maybe you're not the Incredible Hulk – more his alter ego, what's his name?"

"David Banner."

"That's it, David Banner."

"So, after working out like crazy I only have the arms of a wimpy scientist?"

"But... an *adult's* wimpy arms."

"Thanks a lot, dad."

CHAPTER 9

Neil was as physically ready as he was ever going to be when baseball practice opened on the second Saturday of March. Mentally, it was another story. Neil was wound tighter than a newly stitched baseball, so keyed up that he barely slept the night before.

"So, what'd you do last night?" Jon asked Neil, as the two sat together in the bleachers of the East Hill auxiliary gymnasium.

"Nothing much," answered Neil, nervously scrunching up his mitt, as if the old, broken-in-glove could possibly be loosened any more. "Watched a little TV. You?"

"I watched the *Facts of Life.*"

"The *Facts of Life?!* You're kidding, right? I'd rather watch *"The History of the English Language,"* or whatever it was that my dad was watching on PBS last night, than that."

"What'd you watch?"

"*The Battle of the Network Stars.*"

"How was that?"

"It was okay."

"Which network won?"

"I don't remember. I didn't recognize a lot of the actors. Gabe Kaplan wasn't even on this year."

"Remember that year when he smoked Robert Conrad in a foot race?"

"That was great. Who knew "Mr. Kotter" could run like that? Conrad was running like he had a battery from his commercial on his shoulder and didn't want it to fall off."

"Hey, wanna come over tonight and watch the Knicks game?"

"Who're they playing?"

"Celtics."

"Yeah, that'd be good...

"It's ten after 8:00 already. Man, where are the coaches?"

"Maybe they're still in bed, sleeping, like Marc is."

"I think he's the only freshman who's not trying out. Doesn't it seem like there's a lot of kids here?"

"There's sure a lot more here than there was for basketball tryouts."

"Yeah, and why are the sophomores here, too? Wouldn't the junior varsity practice separately, like in basketball? I hope they're not going to combine the teams. That wouldn't be good for us."

"Why would they do that?"

"Maybe the school can't afford a freshman and jayvee team. I don't know."

"Don't be paranoid. East Hill could afford to field *two* freshman teams, if it wanted to."

Waiting for practice to begin, Neil couldn't help but steal uneasy looks around the gym looking for Thorne. He'd seen little of the teen since the new year began; they didn't have a class together that semester and Neil purposely gave Thorne a wide berth – not sitting within ten tables of him and his clique in the lunch room ever since he and Jon's ill-fated decision to eat with them that fall day.

Neil hadn't heard any more about Thorne trying out for the baseball team since running into Dave Cavenall six weeks ago. But he hadn't been actively inquiring about Thorne either. Much like Neil had ignored the weaknesses in his basketball game and assumed they'd go away on their own, he hoped the talk about Thorne being a great center fielder was just a rumor. Now, with the opening of baseball tryouts just minutes away, Neil finally allowed himself to acknowledge that Thorne still existed.

Looking around the gym, Neil spotted Thorne across the court on the opposite bleachers – the center of attention as usual – talking to a group of freshmen and sophomores. As repulsed as Neil was at the sight of Thorne, for all the negative history that the bully triggered in his head, he couldn't look way. *Amazing*, Neil said to himself, with a touch of envy and awe. Thorne had an air about him and a commanding presence that even made him popular with older kids. Fresh off personally successful football and basketball seasons, Thorne looked more relaxed and secure than any teenager had a right to be, no doubt believing that the starting center field job on the freshman baseball team – the hat-trick on his storybook athletic year – was in the bag.

Watching how Thorne confidently carried himself, Neil was struck as to how much older the teen seemed to be than most of the other ninth graders, himself included. Thorne was fourteen, maybe fifteen, but at about 6'0" and a solid 170 or so pounds, he could easily pass for seventeen or eighteen. Thorne looked like he even shaved regularly – something the peach-fuzz faced Neil was still at least a couple years away from doing.

And for someone who was about to get dirty and sweaty over the next couple hours, Thorne looked immaculately well groomed, as if he'd just come from a modeling shoot. Not a hair of his blonde mane was out of place. Stylishly feathered back and parted down the middle, he looked like East Hill's answer to Shaun Cassidy. Neil, on the other hand, who wouldn't even think of using a blow dryer – even on sub-zero temperature days – had half heartedly tried to flatten down his unruly bed head that morning with a wet hairbrush before considering it a lost cause and burying his locks under a scuffed up, mail order San Francisco Giants cap.

Neil couldn't imagine Thorne having to answer to *any* authority figure – be it a teacher, coach or even his own parents. Nor could he picture Thorne having to do something as un-cool as go back-to-school shopping with his mother or perform household chores. *I bet he even calls his folks by their first names,* Neil said to himself.

The contrasts between the two teenagers – physically, socially and economically – couldn't have been more pronounced. Thorne's skin was smooth and clear and his teeth were naturally rail straight and white; by contrast, the acne on Neil's face formed the shape of the Big Dipper and the inside of his mouth seemed to hold more hardware than an Erector Set; Thorne was physically imposing; Neil was about as intimidating as Jimmy Carter was to Ayatollah Khomeini; Thorne got laid (or so Neil assumed). Neil had only a vague idea of what getting to first base meant; Thorne partied. Neil didn't know "party" could be used as a verb; and Thorne's family owned two homes, while Neil's had two mortgages on one house.

~~~

Snapping out of his daydream and finally able to break away from his target, Neil said to no one in particular, "God, I just wish they'd start practice *alrea...*"

"Sorry we're late, guys," interrupted a booming voice from the court. "We had to get some last-minute details squared away. Can I have everyone move to the north bleachers, please?"

Every boy's head turned to see Coach Preece, dressed in a buttoned up red windbreaker, with matching-colored East Hill baseball cap and baggy gray sweatpants, walking swiftly across the court. He was followed by a shorter man, clad in the same, color-coordinated outfit, and two clipboard-toting student managers.

Neil had never seen this second coach before, but unless the man had undergone a dramatic physical metamorphosis in the past several months, he knew it wasn't Krotzen. With a pear-shaped body and a disproportionately sized small head that appeared even tinier due to his large, brown-framed glasses, the bookish-looking man cut a nerdy profile that seemed more accountant than baseball coach. Standing next to the athletic-looking Preece, the identically dressed man looked like the "after" to Preece's "before" in a weight-loss ad.

Preece proceeded to launch into virtually the same introductory speech he'd recited four months earlier at the start of basketball tryouts, only this time substituting "baseball" in for the "basketball" references. The coach then went on to address one of the two nagging questions Neil had on his mind that morning.

"You may be wondering why both the prospective junior varsity and freshman teams are here together," Preece continued. "The reason is because there's considerably more boys who are trying out for the freshman team than the junior varsity team, so we're going to combine the two squads for the two-week tryout period. This will allow me to help Coach Heliver, who will be coaching the freshman team, to evaluate who should make his club."

From his seat on the bleachers, Thorne raised his hand.

"Mr. Thorne, you have something to say?" inquired Preece, pointing to the youth.

"Yeah, coach, where's Coach Krotzen?" asked Thorne, voicing the other question Neil had. "I thought he was going to be the freshman team's coach?"

"I was going to get to that," answered Preece, looking uneasily at his feet. "That's why we're a little late getting started. Coach Heliver and I had to iron out a game plan here at the eleventh hour. Yes, Coach Krotzen was supposed to be the head coach for the freshman team and Coach Heliver his assistant, but we learned this morning that Coach Krotzen won't be coaching this season after all. He's going to be out on disability leave for a while. So, in his absence, Coach Heliver will run the freshman team.

"Are their any more questions? No? Okay, we'll hold practice every day but Sundays and the rosters will be announced on Friday, the 28th. We'll meet here every day after school at 3:00 for stretching exercises and to discuss that day's agenda. Then, weather permitting, we'll move things outside – as we'll do today because it's pretty mild – to the two adjoining diamonds on the lower field; the varsity will be practicing separately on the top field. If the weather doesn't cooperate, we can do nearly everything we'd like to do in here and in the wrestling gym where the batting cage is set up. Coach Heliver, would you like to say a few words?"

"Thanks, coach," said the portly man, opening a frighteningly large mouth that seemed to hold quite a bit more than the standard thirty two teeth found in the human skull. "I'll tell you a little bit about my background. Like Coach Preece, this is also my first year coaching baseball at East Hill. I also teach AP Biology here, so I'll probably be seeing some or most of you in the classroom in the coming years. For the past six years I've been an assistant baseball coach for the freshman and then the jayvee baseball teams in Moonachie.

"I know you freshmen were expecting Coach Krotzen to be your coach, but I can assure you that we won't miss a beat. While I've never been a head coach before, my teams never had a losing record and I expect to continue that streak this season.

One thing I can add to Coach Preece's remarks is that we're going to be looking for fundamentally sound ballplayers. That, and guys who are heady, hustle and have good attitudes. So, coach, should we get to it?"

"Let's do it," said Preece, clapping his hands once. "Everyone come out on the court and find a spot to stretch."

"Can you believe it, Brick?" said Jon excitedly, as the boys climbed down from the bleachers. "No Krotzen."

111

"I know," whispered Neil. "This is great. I don't know what this coach is like, but he can't possibly be any worse than Krotzen was. Tryouts are already going better than any part of basketball practice."

~~~

After stretching, the players changed into their cleats and followed the coaches out to the first baseball diamond on the lower ball field. There, Preece addressed the group again.

"The schedule each day for outdoor practice will be as follows: After we stretch in the gym, we'll come out and loosen up by playing catch for ten minutes," he said. "Then, we'll divide up. Coach Heliver will take the infielders and catchers to the far field and work through defensive drills, and I'll take the outfielders and work with them. Then, we'll have batting practice, run through some base-running situations and finish up with sprints. The forecast so far looks pretty good for Monday, so I suspect we'll be outside again and we'll start working in some intra squad scrimmages then.

"One more thing: if any of you are torn about defensive positions, just try out for the one you want to play. We can't promise you you'll end up there because we may, after seeing you play, think you'd be better suited to another position. But, at least in the beginning, go to the position where you're most comfortable. Right now, pick a throwing partner and one of you grab a ball from the bin on the pitcher's mound here. Half of you line up along the third base line; your partners will spread out along the infield and outfield."

Reflexively, Neil – with Jon following, after he'd retrieved a ball – jogged toward the outfield. When Neil got as far as third base, though, he stopped in his tracks.

"What're you doing?" asked Jon. "We're supposed to be warming up."

"Let's throw by the mound, instead," Neil told his friend.

"Why? What difference does it make where we throw? It's just warm ups? Who cares?"

"I do. I wanna be in front of the coaches. There's too many kids here. I have to stand out."

"*You*, want to stand out?! The wallflower at every school dance?!"

"Hey, fellas, are you going to throw or talk?" yelled Preece to Neil and Jon. "C'mon, let's go."

"That's one way to stand out," quipped Jon to Neil, as the pair ran back towards the middle of the diamond.

Carving out a spot by the pitcher's mound, Neil proceeded to throw darts to Jon; hard and fast throws that popped loudly and painfully in the palm of Jon's mitt, when his friend was unfortunate enough not to catch them in the glove's webbing.

"Okay, outfielders stay with me," yelled out Preece, after about ten minutes of the players throwing. "Everyone else, follow Coach Heliver to the other field."

"Five, ten, fifteen, sixteen outfielders, it looks like we have," counted out Preece, when the infielders, including prospective third baseman, Jon, left the field. "Raise your hand if you're a sophomore. Okay, that's six. Freshmen and sophomores, I'll be learning your names as we go along – if I don't know them already. In the meantime, Freddy Garrett, the jayvee manager here, will be helping me keep track of you. He probably knows more of you than I do, and will record notes I give him. I'll move guys to different positions in the outfield in the next few practices, but for right now, we'll have everybody go to center. Line up in single file. I'll hit you each one ball at a time – grounder, line drive or high fly – and you'll throw them in to Freddy, as if you're trying to cut down a runner at home plate. Then you'll rotate to the back of the line. Okay, go."

The boys jogged to center field and jockeyed for position – Neil lining up near the front. While waiting his turn to field, Neil sized up his competition. He figured no more than half of the ten freshmen outfielders would make the team. While Neil didn't want to underestimate anyone, he knew if he played up to his ability that he'd beat out the three kids at practice who he knew from Eastham Elementary. That left six fellow competitors from Woodbridge – Thorne included – whose talents were as yet unknown to him.

"Ready?" yelled Preece, when Neil's chance came up.

Neil signaled he was by raising his gloved hand and Preece swung the fungo bat, cracking a sharp grounder up the middle. Neil charged the ball. Anticipating where it would bounce, he leaned over and put his glove to the grass. As he did, the ball took a bad hop off a divot and came up to Neil quicker and higher than he expected. Late to adjust to its new trajectory and speed, the ball hit the heel of Neil's glove, popped sharply into the air and dribbled away. Recovering quickly, Neil barehanded the ball and fired it back on a line into home plate. Skipping like a stone on a pond, it bounced once just shy of the pitcher's mound and then

114

caromed a second time some fifteen feet later before losing speed and trickling weakly into the student manager's mitt.

"Nice play, man," cracked Thorne, as Neil bowed his head and passed him on his way to the end of the line.

Crap, Neil said to himself. *Nice first impression.* Neil knew that Preece was too far away to detect that the ball had taken a bad hop; all the coach could tell was that Neil had muffed the play.

Looking up from his feet, Neil saw Preece turn and talk to the student manager, who then dropped his mitt and began scribbling on his clipboard. From two hundred feet away, Neil could predict what the boy, a sophomore who he knew from town, was recording on his scouting report: "Bricker: bad hands, weak arm."

Two players later, Neil watched Thorne catch a fly ball and unleash a perfect strike to home plate. The throw drew a near-collective gasp from the other outfielders – except for a dismayed Neil, who slightly shook his head, while wondering if there was anything Thorne couldn't do.

Neil had five more chances in the fielding drill, all of which he handled flawlessly. But so did Thorne, who continued to show off his superior throwing arm. As the group moved to the infield for base running practice, Neil checked off the mental scorecard he was keeping in his head. As biased as he was, even Neil had to admit that round one in their fight for the center field job, had to go to Thorne.

CHAPTER 10

"Now, we're going to practice reading a pitcher's windup," said Preece, toeing the pitching rubber, after the players finished shagging balls in the outfield. "I'll do some deliveries to the plate and mix in some pickoff attempts – first as a right-handed pitcher and then as a lefty. I'll just motion over to first or home rather than throw. Let's do this in two groups. The eight closest to me right now can go first. Start on the first base line – lining up at the bag and behind it – and take your leads. If I throw to home, run to second. If not, then return to the line and the next group will take their turn."

As a member of the second group, Neil stood aside and studied Preece's delivery. On his first "throw" to the plate, Preece's windup fooled no one. All of the kids in the first group, including Thorne, immediately broke in the direction of second base, with Thorne unnecessarily sliding head first into the bag.

"Good hustle, Bobby," said Preece. "No victims on that move. Guess I'll have to break out my 'A' pickoff move now. Next up."

Neil took a position along the first base line – ahead of the seven other outfielders in his group – while Preece assumed a left-hander's motion. Working from the stretch position, the coach leaned back on his left leg and curled his right leg over his left knee. As Preece swung his right foot around, Neil broke for second base, head down, legs churning hard across the infield dirt.

"Got you!" yelled Preece, his words stopping Neil dead in his tracks midway between first and second base. "I went to first base, not home plate."

Looking around, Neil saw that he was alone on the base path. None of the other boys, who by now were returning to the first base line, had been fooled by the coach's delivery. Feeling embarrassed and stupid, Neil wished the base path would swallow him up like quicksand. He was certain the coach's leg had been moving towards home plate and not first base. But if that was the case, then he was the only one in his group who saw it.

"Hey, don't stop running!" continued Preece. "You're out for sure if you stop. Hey, guys, even if you get picked off, run it out and make the defense make a play on you. Never quit on a play. Let's do that again with the guys who are left from that group."

So much for playing heads up ball, Neil thought.

When it was Neil's group's turn to repeat the drill, he briefly considered lining up in the middle, to melt within the crowd and "cheat" by seeing what the kids in front of him would do first. Then Neil at least wouldn't be left out on an island if he got picked off again. But going against his instincts, the teen took a position at the head of the line. *Shame on me,* he said to himself, *if I let one mistake erase all the hard work I've done. Better to get picked off again, then to hide. Show him you're better than that. And this time, don't be in such a hurry. Watch Preece's move all the way.*

Switching back to a right-handed delivery, Preece peered over his left shoulder at the runners leading off of first base, looked away, then quickly rotated his body and simulated a throw towards the bag. Watching the coach's left leg the whole time, Neil saw it move to first and returned to the base; half the other runners didn't, breaking instead for second base. When the remaining players took another lead, Preece went into his motion again and this time delivered to home plate. Neil broke for second as soon as he saw the coach's left leg plant in front of the mound, and easily outran the rest of his competitors.

Not bad, Neil told himself, *but there's really no excuse to get picked off by a right-hander; lefty pitchers' pickoff moves are much tougher to read.*

Neil knew how he faired against a left-hander would be the *real* measure of his base-running ability in Preece's eyes. Eager for his chance at redemption against Preece, the left-hander, Neil again stepped to the front for his group's next turn. Measuring his lead to four steps – just long enough to allow him to safely return to the base in the event of a pickoff attempt – he carefully examined Preece's motion. This time, the coach cocked his head and paused slightly in his windup, causing seven of the runners to retreat to first. Neil, however, seeing Preece's right leg pass the point of no return that would have resulted in a balk had he thrown to first base, broke for second. The coach continued with his delivery to home plate. Neil hadn't fallen for the move. Pete Townshend, writer of the Who's iconic hit, "Won't Get Fooled Again," would have been proud of him.

"Good work. Let's move on to some B.P., some batting practice, now," said Preece, after running the pickoff drill a few more times – all of which Neil completed successfully. "Bobby Thorne, you can start us off. Grab a helmet and take some warm-up swings, while Freddy sets up the screen in front of the mound. Scotty Wagner, you'll be on deck. For the rest of you, we have fourteen fielders and only seven positions, so just fan out around the field. After every batter you'll move over one position to your left. We'll rotate a new guy in every ten or so swings, starting with the first baseman."

Settling into a seam between left and center field, Neil watched Thorne Velcro seal his new batting gloves and spit on the ground before entering the batter's box. Batting right-handed, Thorne held his shimmering, new aluminum bat at the handle and cocked it menacingly behind his right ear. Preece went into his delivery and threw a low fastball over the heart of the plate. Thorne took a mighty uppercut and rocketed a deep fly ball towards the left-field fence. Neil immediately turned and gave chase. Quickly judging its flight and speed, he took the correct angle and was gaining on the ball as it began to make its descent. Eyes fixed on the target, Neil could practically see the stitches on it as the ball hurtled toward him.

"Mine, mine, mine," yelled Neil, calling for the ball when he spotted the advancing left fielder out of the corner of his eye.

Neil was only yards away from making a great running catch – the kind Preece would no doubt be impressed by. Reaching his gloved left hand high overhead, a still-sprinting Neil jumped off his right leg to get more extension. Opening his glove wide, the ball ice cream coned high in the webbing, just as he ran out of real estate – his right side meeting the hard metal bar that ran horizontally atop the four-foot-high home run fence. But unlike the fence, Neil's body gave. The force of the impact bent him violently in half – his upper body stretching over the fence. Thrown in reverse, as if yanked by an invisible cord, Neil landed flat on his back on the cold, hard outfield grass.

"You okay, man?" asked the left fielder, a Woodbridge kid, sinking to one knee to check on Neil's condition.

"I think so," answered Neil, momentarily stunned by the collision and clutching his right side in pain.

"You're lucky that was a chain fence and not a regular wall," said the boy, helping Neil to his feet. "Did you even look at the fence once?"

"Where's the ball?" asked Neil, not finding it in his glove nor seeing it on the field.

"It popped out of your mitt and over the fence. It was a home run. A typical Thorne shot. The kid's a frickin' monster."

"Everything okay out there?" yelled a concerned Preece from the pitcher's mound, cupping his bare hand and mitt to his mouth.

Bent over at the knees and wincing, Neil raised his gloved hand to acknowledge that he was fine. Figuring the coach was probably less than convinced, though, Neil started to walk off the hurt, settled back into his defensive stance, raised his glove once more and hoped that Thorne wouldn't hit another ball his way until he felt well enough to run without limping.

Apparently satisfied, Preece turned back towards home plate to resume throwing batting practice and delivered another fastball – this one on the inside corner, which Thorne promptly ripped in fair territory on a line past the third basemen and on one hop to the left fielder.

What a shot, Neil said to himself. *Is their anything this jerk can't do?* Three pitches and three hard hit balls into left field later, Preece turned the palm of his mitt up, indicating to Thorne that his next delivery would be a curveball. Snapping off a perfect hook, Preece's pitch started at Thorne's head. As it broke towards the middle of the plate, the youth set his lead left foot toward third base, rather than the pitcher's mound, swung away and missed the ball by several inches.

Again the coach gestured that a curve was coming, then threw a sharp, low-breaking pitch that Thorne chased into the dirt on the outside part of the plate. Angered at his inept swing, the youth flung the bat down on the plate.

"Hey, Bobby, pick the bat up and relax," called out Preece, loud enough for Neil to hear in the outfield. "You've got three more swings left. Now, bear down."

Preece tossed another curve. Thorne followed it all the way and pulled a grounder through the hole between shortstop and third base. *About time he hit one,* Neil thought, running stiffly over to field the ball, before throwing it back to the infield. *It's only the third pitch in a row that he's known a curve has been coming.* His composure regained, Thorne finished out the round pounding two line drives into the left-field corner.

With ten kids in front of him before he could bat, and Preece losing more of his self-control with each batter, a shivering and restless Neil slowly worked his way around the field, trying to stay loose, while watching the strawberry-colored bruise above his right hip ripen.

Finally, a half hour after batting practice began, Neil moved to the on-deck circle. If there was one good thing, he thought, to come out of being one of the last to hit, it was that his banged-up hip wasn't as sore anymore. Donning a batting helmet, he tested the weight of several aluminum bats before finding one that felt light enough for him to maintain good bat control.

"What's going on, Brick?" asked Freddy, the team manager, moving over to the bat rack where Neil was warming up.

121

"How's things, Freddy?" answered Neil, slipping a weighted donut over his bat.

"What position are you trying out for?"

"Center field."

"So's Thorne, the kid from Woodbridge."

"Yeah, I know."

"You sure you don't want me to put you down for another position? Maybe left field or right?"

"No, thanks. I'll stick with center."

"Okay. Well, just trying to help. Good luck."

Swinging his weighted bat, Neil was irritated that a boy he'd grown up with and who knew how well he could play, was already writing him off in the competition for starting center fielder.

"Next batter," called Preece, when the boy in front of Neil had finished taking his cuts at the plate.

Pawing the back of the right-handed batter's box with his right cleat, Neil settled into his stance and waited for Preece's first pitch. Going into a full windup, the coach threw an eye-high fastball down the middle of the plate – too high, but also too tempting to pass up. With his adrenaline flowing like water released from an uncoiled garden hose, an overanxious Neil swung through the pitch for a strike.

Stepping back out of the batter's box, he bent down to scoop up a handful of dirt and rubbed it up and down the handle of his bat, like he'd seen New York Yankees outfielder Lou Piniella do dozens of times on TV. Taking two deep breaths, Neil got back into the box and reset his feet. *Wait for your pitch, idiot*, he demanded of himself. *Don't forget who you are. You're a contact hitter. Choke up a little more and just try to hit the ball hard. Don't try to kill it.*

Preece's next delivery was another fastball, which Neil promptly returned, nailing a line drive into the protective screen in front of the mound. Preece ducked and flinched as a natural reflex. *Up the middle. Perfect. That'll get the coach's attention*, Neil said to himself.

Tapping his bat on the plate, Neil readied for Preece's third pitch. The ball left Preece's hand and veered to the outside corner of the plate. Still a strike, Neil went with the pitch and hit a hard grounder through the hole between first and second base into right field. Now into a groove, with two good hits in a row, Neil either smacked the next four pitches sharply on the ground or as line drives into the outfield – most likely singles, had they been hit in an actual game.

"Curves coming on the last three," shouted Preece, doffing his glove hand and winding up for the next pitch in Neil's round. The ball started out in the direction of Neil's head, but knowing what pitch was coming, he waited for it to break into the strike zone. When it did, Neil swung – albeit a hair too late, hitting a foul ball behind home plate. The next curve was also a strike, but Neil pulled it weakly on the ground to the third baseman. "Not what you're supposed to do," he muttered softly. "Hit it where it's pitched." The last pitch also broke on the outside part of the plate. Self-correcting from the previous delivery, Neil served a solid line drive that bounced once in front of the right fielder.

"Nice job," said Preece to Neil. "Next – and last – batter, right, Freddy?"

Neil discarded his helmet and bat, retrieved his hat and glove and sprinted to the outfield, the coach's compliment adding an extra spring to his step. It was the first pat on the back he'd received from a coach since he'd run on the cross country team in the fall, but infinitely more meaningful given that Neil only participated in track and field to pass the time until basketball tryouts. With batters failing, on the average, much more than they succeed, Neil had managed to hit the ball on the screws more than half the time in his round of B.P. Those harsh, solitary winter days of hitting ball after ball into the paint tarp in the boathouse seemed to be paying dividends for him right off the bat.

~~~

"Not a bad first practice, I'd say," said Preece, calling his group onto the pitcher's mound after the last outfielder took his cuts. "We have a lot of work to do on fundamentals, but that's to be expected. Let's finish up with sprints – ten of them, with thirty-second rests in between. You'll start on the left-field line and finish in center where Freddy will be stationed."

Most of the boys – either tired from the practice or conserving energy – ran the sprints at half speed. Neil didn't get that memo. He had no intention of pacing himself. Running through the pain in his hip, he won the first leg, beating freshmen and sophomores. Neil scorched the field again in the next two races.

"Hey...Edwin Moses...slow the hell up," called out Thorne, between heavy breaths, walking back to the finish line with hands on his hips awaiting the next sprint. "What, are you trying out for the Olympics, or something? You're making us all look bad. These sprints don't mean nothing. They're not gonna help you make the team. If everyone runs the same medium speed no one will get in trouble. Catch my drift?"

Neil ignored Thorne's "advice" and lined up next to the student manager. Seconds later he was off again – chugging hard and ahead of the pack.

I didn't run every day for the last six weeks to make anyone else, especially Thorne, look good, Neil said to himself, as he lengthened his lead. *It's not my problem if they can't keep up with me.*

Neil won the next six races going away. For the last sprint, Thorne lined up facing Neil rather than at his back.

"I *said...* slow... down," hissed Thorne, huffing and puffing softly between words, his intense, piercing blue eyes trying to burn a hole through Neil's face.

Breathing only slightly harder than he was after the first sprint, Neil turned a deaf ear.

"Go!" yelled Freddy.

The irritated Thorne was running more purposefully now and stayed with Neil for the first dozen yards, determined to beat him. But too tired to challenge for the duration, he soon dropped back to the pack, as Neil cruised to another win and a clean sweep in the sprints.

"Looks like we'll have to work on developing stamina with some of you," said Preece to the outfielders, many of whom were bent over at the waist with their hands on their knees, gulping air from having to run faster than they wanted to in a vane attempt to keep pace with Neil. "Don't forget, we meet in the auxiliary gym Monday at 3:00. We'll see what the weather brings and then go from there."

Neil – mindful of the potential consequences of crossing Thorne – quickly gathered up his hat and glove and jogged ahead of the others back across the empty teacher's parking lot and into the school. A few feet later he turned into the locker room and pulled up alongside his locker.

Other than verbal intimidation, Thorne could do little to Neil on the field with Preece present, but Neil knew from firsthand experience what the bully was capable of doing absent of adult supervision.

"Aren't you gonna shower?" asked Jon, who was already sitting half dressed in front of his locker, the infielders having finished a few minutes before the outfielders.

"I'll shower at home, c'mon," answered Neil hurriedly, plucking his street clothes out of his locker."

"What's the big rush?"

"Just c'mon. I'll tell you when we get outta here. Get dressed."

Pulling his still laced-up cleats off his feet and shoving them into his gym bag, alongside the street clothes, Neil had almost finished tying his sneakers when he heard the click-clack of the outfielders' cleats echoing loudly in the hallway outside.

"Let's go," said Neil, grabbing his gym bag. With the puzzled Jon following close behind, Neil wove his way through the maze of lockers and ducked out a side door that led into the wrestling gym. Two more exits later and the boys were safely outside, home free.

"*Now* can you tell me what that was all about?" asked Jon, tucking his flannel shirttail into his pants.

"I was running too fast for Thorne in the sprints and showing everyone up, I guess," said Neil, panting and sweating more from the last few anxiety-filled moments than he had during all of the ninety-minute practice.

"So…"

"So, I'm not taking any chances with him. Not after what happened during basketball tryouts."

"Sounds like you had an interesting practice. Was it good?"

"Yeah. Not bad. I hit okay. What'd the infielders do?"

"Everything you did, probably, just we took infield practice instead of outfield practice. After awhile, the sophomores got bored and started using the student manager for target practice."

"What do you mean, target practice?"

"They'd field a ball hit by the coach then throw it back in to the manager. Except, they'd purposely short hop it so it would come up and hit him. You'd get one point if it him in the chest, arm or leg, two for anything that struck him in the head or face and three if it nailed him in the balls. The poor kid didn't know what was going on."

"Any balls hit him in the nuts?"

"Just one. Mostly, they got 'em in the legs."

"That's still one too many. Did you play it?"

"I won, but I wasn't really playing."

"Whadda you mean? How can you win if you don't play?"

"Well…one of my throws *accidentally* short hopped him and got 'em in the nuts. That was worth three points, which was more than anyone else had."

"Wonder what's up with Krotzen?" asked Neil, after he'd stopped laughing at his friend. "Why do you think he's all of a sudden not coaching? Not like I'm complaining."

"Not sure," replied Jon, "but I overheard a couple of the sophomores talking about it. They said the student manager from Woodbridge… the one who got hit in the grapes…"

"You mean, the one *you* hit in the grapes?"

"Yeah, that one. Well, he told 'em that Krotzen got into a fight with his wife last night. She beat the crap out of him. Messed him up really good. He's in the hospital; broken jaw, arm and a concussion."

"Too bad he didn't have his football team buddies there for protection."

CHAPTER 11

Monday's practice was also held outside. Picking up where he left off on Saturday, Neil played it smarter in the pickoff drill, making positively sure that the coach was committed to a move to home plate or first base before breaking for second base, or returning to the bag. Neil also played it safe when it came to being around Thorne. Not wanting to risk getting cornered by him in the locker room, Neil never gave Thorne the chance. Instead, he changed for practice in a boy's bathroom on the other side of school, then stowed his street clothes in his regular locker.

In subsequent practices and intra-squad scrimmages that week Thorne was still hitting the ball – on those rare occasions when he made contact – as if his aluminum bat was corked. But for every long shot he clubbed, Thorne would overswing and miss on ten pitches. And for every time he made a perfect throw to the plate from center field, he'd sail a handful over a cutoff man's head.

Thorne could have all the style points he wanted, concluded Neil. In the meantime, Neil would quietly and methodically go about his business, gathering the substance ones that the coaches wanted to see, like advancing runners when he was at the plate, laying down perfect sacrifice bunts, and making up for his relatively weak arm by always hitting the cutoff man and hustling like a rabid dog.

Still shy around his peers, Neil rarely said a word at practice, other than to call for a ball in the outfield, but he didn't have to say much. Neil felt like his actions on the field were speaking far louder than any inane rah-rah chatter could.

When the first week of tryouts ended, Neil felt like he was pulling away from Thorne in their competition. Thorne seemed to sense it, too. Challenged athletically for perhaps the first time in his life, the Woodbridge youth grew increasingly frustrated by his mistakes, taking his aggression out on bats, helmets – whatever innocent inanimate, object happened to be in his way. Thorne was succumbing to the pressure, emotionally unraveling like a baseball after its cover's been torn off.

~~~

The halfway point of tryouts coincided with Jon's fifteenth birthday. That Saturday night, while many of their classmates partied, Jon celebrated by inviting Neil to attend a New York Knicks game with he and his father at Madison Square Garden in midtown Manhattan. Arriving home an hour after the game ended, Neil found his father asleep in his easy chair in the parlor with the TV on.

"Dad, why don't you go up to bed?" said Neil, gently shaking his sleeping father's shoulder.

"What time is it?" asked a groggy Al, wiping his left hand down his face.

"About 11:15."

"How was the game?"

"Great, but the Bullets won 122-113. The Bullets starting forwards outscored the Knicks starting forwards fifty nine to eighteen."

"Only you would know that breakdown – much less care. Tough to win with that type of production. Seems like a hundred years ago that the Knicks were last any good."

"Any more Olympics news?" asked Neil, for about the tenth time that day, referring to President Carter's announcement that afternoon that the U.S. would boycott the upcoming summer games.

"Nope. And I wouldn't expect any either," said Al, unfolding his frame from the chair and stretching out his stiff lower back. "Carter's not going to reverse his stance on the boycott. If he did he'd look like an even more impotent president than he already is. Too bad, too. Athletes shouldn't be used as pawns in diplomatic affairs. That boycott's not going to accomplish a damn thing other than to let the Soviets clean up in medals. So ends my foreign affairs lecture for the evening. I'm going to bed. Did you lock up?"

"Yeah, I did after I came in."

"Unlock it. I don't think Marc's home yet."

"You're not gonna wait up for him?"

"No, he's a big boy. He can take care of himself. See you in the morning."

Too keyed up from the Knicks game to turn in and with the TV all to himself for a change, Neil grabbed a box of Nilla Wafers from the kitchen cupboard and mixed up a glass of Tang. Returning to the parlor, he kicked off his Pumas and settled into his father's warm chair. Neil's timing was impeccable. Coming out of a commercial break, WNBC TV, Channel 4's sports report led off with highlights of the Knicks-Bullets game. Sitting up in his chair to get a closer look at the screen, Neil watched the recap as if he hadn't just seen the game in person or had any idea of the outcome.

When the channel's highlights ended, Neil got up from his seat and quickly snapped the dial on the TV to Channel 2 to catch WCBS' sports report, knowing that the reports for the three major networks' tri-state newscasts were never in perfect synch. Neil was right, but he only saw about ten seconds of game highlights before the broadcast segued into news from the Yankees spring training camp. With one more network left to try, Neil moved up the dial, turning the knob on the set to Channel 7. But when he got there, Neil knew immediately that he'd missed the Knicks highlights. WABC was already onto its hockey coverage. Despite the New York Islanders' and Rangers' successes in recent seasons, the fourteen year old was sports savvy enough to know that New York was still a basketball town in March – no matter how far out of contention the Knicks happened to be – so none of the area networks would ever lead off their sports reports with hockey highlights.

Shortly before 11:30, Neil switched back to WNBC. *Saturday Night Live* would be airing shortly and Neil never missed a show – even in a season when the groundbreaking program was clearly in decline, absent the star power of former cast members John Belushi and Dan Aykroyd, who'd left to act in feature films.

Much to his chagrin, however, *SNL* was a re-run that week. Getting up from his seat, Neil made a few revolutions of the TV dial to check what else was on. He worked it to the left and then back to the right as if the knob was a combination lock, before finally returning to Channel 4 and the *SNL* repeat.

132

Vacantly staring at the screen, his face expressionless through the lame jokes and skits, Neil munched non-stop on cookies through two commercial breaks before hearing the back door open and close. Moments later, Marc stood before him in the parlor.

"What's up?" asked Marc, ripping the box of Nilla Wafers out of his brother's hands.

"Hey, what gives?" asked an irritated Neil. "You coulda asked first…I'd have given it to you."

"So sue me, I'm starving," mumbled Marc, spitting out crumbs onto the floor as he talked.

"You better clean that up or mom'll be pissed when she sees it."

"*You* pick 'em up."

"*You* did it! *You* clean it up! Man, you reek," said Neil, shielding his nose with his hand to block the offensive smell of tobacco mixed with the Hai Karate aftershave lotion Marc seemingly bathed in before going out that night. "What'd you *do* tonight?"

"Not too much, smoked a little dope at the party…and on the car ride home."

"A little? You did more than that. Your eyes are totally bloodshot," said Neil, leaning forward off the recliner to get a closer look at Marc's face. "You took a big chance coming in when you did, you know, looking and smelling like that. Dad only went up to bed fifteen minutes ago. He woulda known what you were up to tonight."

133

"No, he wouldn't. He never has before."

"Since when did you turn into Bob Marley? All you do is go to parties and get stoned all the time."

"Bob Marley?! What's that supposed to mean?" Marc asked defensively, picking at the fraying iron-on decal on his Alice Cooper concert t-shirt. "Why am I Bob Marley? Because I'm black?"

"No. I wasn't thinking about that. He's just a famous person who smokes a lot of grass, that's all."

"What do you know about what goes on at parties anymore anyway? All you do on weekends is stay in and watch *Hee Haw*, *The Love Boat*, or some other lame ass show."

Marc's dig touched a raw nerve in Neil. Acutely aware of his outsider social status at East Hill, Neil thought the remark was below the belt and fired back at Marc, who had turned to leave the room, with a rare quick witted and forceful response.

"At least I'm not doing cocaine!" said Neil.

"How'd you know about that?" asked Marc, wheeling around again to face his brother.

"Jon saw you using it at that party last month that you went to on your birthday. What are you thinking, doing that stuff?"

"You're not gonna rat me out to mom and dad, are you?"

His voice rising and cracking with emotion, Neil unleashed the resentment toward Marc that had been building in him since the school year started. Neil proceeded to pummel his brother with one hurtful remark after another.

"Why the hell shouldn't I?" asked Neil, speaking aggressively but in low tones, so as not to risk waking the house. "If I told them, the only parties you'll be allowed to go to will be Gerry's birthday parties. They made all those sacrifices to adopt you – to get you away from Paterson – and the thanks they get is you get mixed up in drugs? Mom and dad have a right to know what you're doing every weekend. They might wonder what the point was in adopting you. Maybe they shouldn't have wasted their time."

"You know…Thorne and the rest of those Woodbridge kids only like you because you're black and live here, don't you? Do you think for one second they'd even *look* at you if they didn't know you and saw you on the street in Paterson? They'd probably cross the street to avoid you. They only like you because you're on their turf and you're the only black kid around. You're safe to them. You're like something they'd bring in to show and tell…something to brag about, so it makes them look cooler to their friends and in front of girls. 'Hey, this is my friend, Marcus. But he wants to be called Marc, so he won't feel so "black."'"

Neil paused from his rant, but not to reflect on what he'd said, only to reload his mouth for another round of spiteful comments.

"And another thing: you wouldn't know Bob Marley anymore from Jacob Marley – that ghost in *A Christmas Carol*. What happened to you? You used to have an afro and watch *Soul Train* and listen to R&B and Hendrix. Now, your hair's shorter than mine and you listen to Steely Dan and Chicago. Ever since you started high school and started hanging around with your new friends, you've acted whiter than me – whiter than those cookies!"

Finally realizing he'd gone too far, Neil stopped talking. But it was too late. The damage had already been done. An awkward, tense silence filled the space between the brothers, creating an odd juxtaposition to the studio audience's laughter at the *SNL* skit currently playing on TV.

For close to a minute Neil and Marc stared uncomfortably at each other, the former suddenly regretting everything he said, yet now unable to speak, much less apologize.

"What do you know about what it's like to be black and to live here?" asked Marc, breaking the silence in a calm, measured tone, before casually flipping the box of cookies back at Neil and stalking from the room.

Marc's words made Neil feel even more ashamed of his tirade. He never intended to bring race into their argument. Neil only wanted to lash out at his brother's drug use, and newfound arrogance, but in the process he'd crossed several lines. And between the lines of what he'd said were his easily readable, hurt feelings over the dissolving of a once solid friendship.

As bad as Neil felt, he knew that his feelings weren't completely unfounded. For better or worse, he was practically the same person he was at fourteen as he was at eight. Whether attributable to nature or nurture, Marc, however, was not. Gone, to Neil, were the qualities that once drew him to his adopted brother: Marc's playfulness, innocence and an ethnicity that made him unique and more interesting than any other kid in town. Now, in speech, appearance and mind-set, Marc was no more of a black kid from Paterson anymore than the stuck-up Woodbridge classmates Neil so loathed.

Nevertheless, Neil realized his outburst was uncalled for and that he had to make amends. Shutting off the TV and the remaining house lights, he went upstairs, quickly brushed his teeth and ascended another flight of stairs to his dark bedroom. Climbing onto his bunk his hand made contact with Marc's pungent, pot-smelling jean jacket hanging on the bedpost. Ten minutes earlier, Neil would have angrily flung the coat on Marc's bed. But calmed down now, he climbed over it and worked his way under the covers. After what he'd said to his brother, Neil rationalized that maybe he deserved the "punishment" of having to breathe in that foul pot scent all night. Propping himself on his elbows, Neil whispered across the room to Marc.

"Marc, you still awake?" asked Neil.

"Uh-huh," came his brother's delayed response from the dark.

"I'm sorry I said what I said. You're right. I…I don't know what it's like to be in your shoes."

"Forget about it, I already did," said Marc, although his edgy tone suggested otherwise.

It had been ages since Neil had issued a sincere, heartfelt apology to *anyone*, for *anything*. Out of practice and unsure as to whether Marc believed him or not, Neil figured his only recourse to prove his earnestness was to repeat the act of contrition – hoping that maybe two perceived half-hearted apologies would equal one genuine confession.

"Okay, well, I'm sorry I said that."

"Yeah, I know."

While he had his brother's attention, Neil wanted to tell Marc more, like how he wished that they were still good friends. But tongue tied by teenaged awkwardness and embarrassment, Neil let the moment pass. The apology had been emotionally draining enough for him.

~~~

The snow that had mixed with rain on Saturday evening continued through much of Sunday, making the second official day of spring feel more like a frigid day in mid January. The temperature wasn't much warmer inside between Neil and Marc – the former's apology failing to fully melt the ice that had built up between them the night before.

By Monday the mercury outside from a weekend of unseasonable cold had inched its way up to about forty degrees. The rising temperature, however, was accompanied by a steady rain, so for the first time since baseball tryouts started, practice was moved indoors.

"I don't care what Preece says, practicing inside isn't *close* to playing outside," said Neil, as he and Jon started their walk home after tryouts that evening.

"It's more dangerous, that's for sure," agreed Jon, holding his gym bag over his head to guard against the rain. "I almost got a ground ball in the face one time. The basketball court's so fast, that the balls pick up speed on every bounce."

"It's boring, too. Everybody's all together and there's less to do, so there's a lot of sitting around. How'd you do hitting off the pitching machine?"

"It took a few pitches to get used to, but okay."

"The wrestling gym was so dark, I couldn't see very well. I've never hit off one of those things before. I couldn't pick up the balls out of those spinning wheels. By the time I got used to it, my round of B.P. was almost over."

"You weren't the only one. Thorne couldn't hit a thing. His meltdown was classic. He was throwing stuff all over the place and swearing."

"That was about the only good thing about today. Thorne can't mess up enough for me."

"You're not still worried about him, are you? You've been doing pretty well so far, right?"

"I think so, but I can't tell if Preece thinks that. He never really says anything positive to anybody – just to the group. Thorne may be messing up, but when he hits it, he's still the best power hitter and he's got a better arm than me. Plus, Preece knows him from football and basketball, so that's got to help him. If he remembers me at all from basketball, it's only because he cut me. Couldn't you see Preece playing favorites and telling Heliver to keep Thorne over me?"

"No. Preece isn't like Krotzen. He's a cool guy. He'll give you a fair shake."

"Maybe, but I can't afford to take anything for granted. Hey, I'm gonna hit some balls off the tee after dinner. Do you wanna come over?'

"I wouldn't go in that crappy, old shed if you paid me. There's probably rats living in there. You hit balls after every practice.

Why don't you take a night off? Come over and watch the Knicks game."

"I can't afford to stop. I know I'm still the underdog. My only chance is to outwork everyone."

~~~

Tuesday dawned almost as cold as Monday, but at least it came without rain. Preece's announcement, though, that fielding and base-running drills would be moved outside – even if it was to only be in the empty teachers' parking lot – considerably brightened Neil's mood.

The fields were still too soggy to play on, however, so batting practice was again held inside. Having finally found his timing on the pitching machine, Neil resumed his torrid batting from the week before, whacking ball after ball hard into the rectangular net that lined the back of the cage. Neil put an exclamation point on his round by smacking a ball that ricocheted off one of the tripod legs that supported the machine – the metal ting bouncing loudly off the four walls in the small gym.

A few batters later, Thorne produced a similar sound when he took his aggression out on his batting helmet, slamming it on the floor after whiffing badly on eight of his ten pitches.

Thorne was still steamed minutes later when the outfielders and Preece gathered on the parking lot for base-running practice.

"It's cold enough out here, so in order to keep you moving and your blood flowing, we'll do the drill with one big group running," said Preece, as Freddy, the student manager, ran around the parking lot dropping rubber bases to form the shape of an infield diamond. "Everybody line up at first base."

Pitching right-handed, Preece worked from the stretch position while the boys took their leads. Winding up, Preece simulated a throw to home plate and the runners bolted for second base. As Neil ran past the bag, the unnatural sound of a body scraping concrete eclipsed the thunder of almost three-dozen pairs of clomping sneakers. Turning around he saw Thorne lying on his back on the pavement, his right leg tucked underneath the extended left leg.

"That was good hustle, Bobby, but a bit unnecessary," called out Preece. "We don't need anyone sliding on concrete today, okay? That's a good way to tear your leg up."

Rising triumphantly to his feet, as if he'd just slid into home plate to score the winning run in an actual game, Thorne ripped off the bottom of his torn right sweatpants leg and held it aloft like a trophy, while accepting low fives from some of the boys – particularly his football teammates – who were awestruck by the youth's macho act.

Who's he kidding? thought Neil, unimpressed with Thorne's grandstanding play. *Krotzen's the only coach who'd be impressed by that cheap, stupid stunt and he ain't here.*

Stunt or not, Thorne's slide on concrete seemed to inspire him. For the rest of the practice he played like a boy possessed, making outstanding running and leaping catches in the parking lot and topping them off with laser-like throws to home plate. Thorne even beat Neil in the end-of-practice sprints – the first time anyone had done so.

CHAPTER 12

By the following afternoon – with just two days remaining until cuts would be announced – the ball fields had drained enough to hold the entire practice outside.

"You guys wouldn't be too upset if we didn't do a regular practice today, would you?" asked Preece, when the infielders and outfielders finished loosening up in the gym. "Today, we're just going to scrimmage for five innings and call it a day. I'll take half the infielders and outfielders for my game and Coach Heliver will take the other half for his game."

When the teams were divided up, Neil and Jon found themselves on the same squad. The opposing club included both the sophomore center fielder, who played on the freshman team the year before, and Thorne, who began the game as their starting pitcher. If Thorne wasn't a lock to make the team as the center fielder, the freshman was, however, a cinch to earn a spot on the roster as a hurler. Although prone to bouts of wildness on the mound, when he was on his game Thorne had an overpowering fastball and a devastating curve – arguably the best stuff of any other freshman pitcher.

Neil had never faced the hard-throwing Thorne before – even during batting practice – when he stepped into the batter's box in the top of the first inning of the scrimmage. Wanting to be able to touch – never mind get around on – a potential Thorne fastball, Neil set up as deep as he could in the batter's box to give himself more time to see and react to the ball.

Thorne's first pitch came in high and hard towards Neil's head. Ducking out of the way, Neil barely avoided the pitch, taking a seat in the dirt as the fastball whizzed past his left temple, over the catcher's mitt and clanged loudly off the metal backstop, the tinny sound moving around the infield like a crisply turned 5-4-3, third to second to first, double play.

"What the hell?" Neil grumbled softly, picking himself up off the ground and brushing the dirt from his sweatpants. "That almost took my head off."

Thorne angrily pounded his fist into his mitt then stood impatiently with hands on hips waiting for the catcher to retrieve the ball. Staring out at the mound, Neil couldn't tell whether Thorne was upset at the pitch getting away from him or because it had failed to connect with Neil's head.

"You all right, Neil?" asked Preece, who was umpiring the scrimmage from behind the mound.

Neil straightened the helmet on his head, nodded that he was okay and stepped back into the batter's box to await Thorne's next delivery.

Once again, the pitch came in high and tight. Still gun shy from the last ball, Neil stepped back out of the way only to helplessly watch it spin away from his body and over the plate for a called first strike.

Neil pawed the hole he'd made in the soft dirt of the batter's box with his right cleat. He knew now that Thorne had set him up by throwing a wild purpose pitch and following it with a knee-buckling curve that Neil wouldn't expect to see.

For the third pitch of the at-bat, Thorne went back to his fastball. The ball rode inside on Neil's fists, but thinking it would still be called a strike, he swung at it anyway, missing it by several inches. Strike two.

Neil looked quizzically at his bat, as if there must be a hole in it, as he rarely swung and missed at a ball. Down in the count, one ball and two strikes, Neil had no more room for error. A confirmed contact hitter from the time his father taught the small boy how to swing a bat, Neil would rather sit through a *Facts of Life* marathon than strike out.

But now he was in great danger of striking out against one of the last people on earth he wanted to give that pleasure to. Mentally preparing himself for what was now a pitcher-batter chess match, Neil knew that Thorne had a couple pitches to play with and waste, if he wanted to. Neil also figured that Thorne had him set up for another curve ball, so he reminded himself that in the event of a hook to hold his ground and not bail out of the batter's box.

Stepping out of the batter's box to take a warm-up swing, Neil quickly recited to himself the memorized checklist his father drummed into him when he first learned to hit; the one he went through before every at-bat: *Pretend like you're chopping wood, so you don't uppercut the ball. Start your swing in a downward motion, with both elbows pointed to the ground. That will keep your swing level. Hit the ball where it's pitched; don't try to muscle up and hit home runs, just try to hit it hard up the middle.*

Neil stepped back into the batter's box. Guessing correctly on Thorne's fourth pitch of the at-bat, Neil let the low and away curveball go for ball two. The next pitch was a fastball that Neil also patiently watched pass out of the strike zone. With the count now full at 3 and 2, Thorne had to come in with something good or he'd put the patient Neil on base with a walk. Knowing this, Neil readied for the safe pitch, the fastball. The pitch most hurlers found the easiest to control. Thorne's payoff pitch came inside and well out of the strike zone to the right-handed swinger, but as Neil relaxed and leaned back out of the way to let it pass for ball four, the ball began to spin back over the plate at his knees. All Neil could do was watch helplessly, as the pitch cut the plate in half. Neil knew he was out on strikes even before Preece raised his right arm to signal the out.

"Yeah!" shouted Thorne, his piercing blue eyes narrowing to slits. The psyched-up youth pounded the palm of his glove with his right hand and stalked around the mound, performing a perfect imitation of Atlanta Braves' relief pitcher Al "The Mad Hungarian" Hrabosky.

Neil dropped his head and walked back to the dugout. Pissed off by his feeble showing at the plate and at being fooled, it took all the self-discipline he could muster not to hurl his bat in frustration. Taking a seat on the bench, Neil couldn't believe that the erratic-throwing Thorne hadn't played the percentages and instead rolled the dice with a curve ball on a full count.

Two innings later when he faced Thorne again, Neil knew it would be a waste of time to try to predict what pitch he'd see on a given count; Thorne was clearly apt to throw any pitch in his repertoire at any time.

Neil wasn't prepared, however, for another high and tight fastball on Thorne's first delivery. Frozen at the plate and unable to duck a wild pitch this time, Neil could only flinch, shut his eyes and brace for the inevitable impact. The pitch struck him flush on the left bicep, with a sound like he'd been whacked across the arm with a two-by-four. Wincing in pain, Neil dropped his bat and immediately pressed his arm tight to his side to somehow try and

145

quell the jellyfish like sting of a hard ball striking flesh on a cold spring day.

"Where'd it get you?" asked a concerned Preece, running from the mound to home plate. "On the elbow?"

"No, just the muscle," answered Neil in a faltering voice, still clutching his forearm.

"At least it hit the meat and not a bone. Can you move it? Do you wanna sit out for a bit?"

"No. I'm okay, coach."

"Sorry, man, it got away from me," Thorne said to Neil, with all the sincerity of a pickup line delivered at last call.

Still smarting, but not wanting to give Thorne the satisfaction of having knocked him out of the scrimmage, Neil jogged to first base. If Neil suspected it during his first at-bat, he was now positive that Thorne was deliberately throwing at him. He could chalk up one wild pitch to an accident but *two* in consecutive at-bats?! Thorne wasn't *that* wild on the mound.

With no action at all in center field over the next couple innings to distract him, Neil continued to stew about his last plate appearance. As he did, unpleasant flashbacks from basketball tryouts came flooding back to him. The at-bat, Neil concluded, was the baseball version of when Thorne shoved him against the hallway locker; different sport, same intention – to intimidate. The more Neil thought about the latest putdown the angrier he got and the more determined he was to get even with Thorne his next time up – assuming he got another crack at him.

The chances of that, however, looked remote, as through the first four innings of the five-inning game, Thorne hadn't given up a run and had only allowed three base runners. With Neil due to bat fourth in the last inning, he needed someone ahead of him to reach base to get his shot at revenge. After striking out the first two batters in the inning, Neil's last hope rested on the ninth-place hitter, Jon, owner of his team's lone base hit. One pitch later, Neil had his chance as Jon solved Thorne again, serving a fastball to center for a single.

His anger cresting, Neil dug in at the batter's box and pounded the barrel of his bat on the plate. Cocking his silver aluminum bat back behind his right ear and crouching into his stance, all Neil could think of was creaming the ball and all he could see was rage red.

Thorne's first pitch of the at-bat came in at eye level. Disregarding the strike zone, Neil swung violently, wildly and missed, so overanxious that he would have waved his bat at a pickoff attempt to first base. Rather than step out of the box to gather his thoughts and composure, Neil's feet stayed fast, as if stuck in cement.

Clearly tiring on the mound, Thorne delivered his second pitch – a fastball in name only. The slower-than-usual delivery had poor location, too, heading right down the middle of the plate at waist level. In baseball terms, it was a textbook meatball and had Neil been in his right frame of mind, he'd have undoubtedly ripped it up the middle for a base hit. But not thinking clearly, Neil swung from his heels – doing the exact opposite of what his father had long ago taught him not to do – missing the pitch by a foot.

Now down to his last strike, Neil was so tense and nervous that the involuntary act of breathing seemed like something he had to remind himself to do. Gripping his bat so tightly that if made of wood it might have been ground to sawdust in his hands, Neil stared out at the mound through tunnel vision eyes. Neil was now in no mental state to discern a dog from a cat, much less a ball from a strike. They all looked like strikes.

With that lack of judgment, Neil never had a chance. The curveball snapped off from Thorne's right hand started out low and inside and then broke into the dirt two feet off the outside corner of the plate. Neil lunged at the pitch – his top hand flying off the bat so as to get greater extension on his swing – but it was no use. He couldn't have hit the pitch with an oar.

"Nice work, Bobby," said Preece after the game-ending strikeout.

The coach popped his index fingers in his mouth and whistled, then waved both teams to join him at the mound.

Trudging to the hill from home plate, Neil intentionally picked a spot deep in the back of the circle of players and knelt low onto the cold ground, hoping that out of sight would translate to out of mind, where Preece was concerned.

"Good pitcher's duel today," the coach continued. "Maybe the hitters will have their day tomorrow when we wrap up the tryouts with another scrimmage. Bobby and Kevin, you guys threw a lot of pitches, so don't forget to ice down your arms tonight."

Preece talked for a few minutes more, but Neil had zoned out after the first three sentences. Now consumed by worry and self-doubt, Neil awakened from his trance only when Preece clapped his hands once to dismiss the players for the day.

After changing clothes in his private locker room in a boy's bathroom near his homeroom, Neil met Jon in front of the school for their walk home. In a good mood from having collected his team's only two hits of the scrimmage, Jon could barely contain his glee. Wanting to relive the game, he thought twice about it and bit his tongue when he saw his dour-faced friend. Five silent minutes passed before Jon broke the ice.

"Can't believe we just have one more practice left," said Jon in a reserved tone. "The two weeks have gone by quick, huh?"

Neil didn't respond.

"Wonder who Preece'll pitch tomorrow," continued Jon.

"They could throw a girl from the softball team and I wouldn't hit it," said Neil dejectedly.

"So, you had one bad practice. You just had an off day, that's all."

"But it was the worst time to have it. I struck out twice. I couldn't hit a frickin' thing today."

"No, *tomorrow* would be the worst time. Hey, Thorne's a tough pitcher. You weren't the only one who had trouble hitting against him. He musta had nine or ten strikeouts today."

"You didn't have any trouble with him."

"I just got lucky."

"That wasn't luck. Those were two clean hits."

"Yeah, well, tomorrow you'll have your stroke back, too."

"I'd better get it back. Right now, I wish tryouts had ended yesterday. Do you think Thorne was purposely throwing at me today? I think he was. After he hit me that second at-bat all I could think of was driving a ball down his throat the next time up. I couldn't see straight anymore."

"Looked intentional to me. He didn't come close to hitting anyone else. I can't believe Preece didn't warn him, or something."

"Are you kidding? He wouldn't say anything. Preece loves him. No way he's not the starting center fielder. After today, I'll just be happy to make the team."

"C'mon. You've outplayed him in almost every practice. How can that not count for something?"

"But he's playing better now and I'm playing worse. Besides, even if all things are equal, Preece will go with Thorne because he knows him from football and basketball."

"I still think it's your job to lose. Plus, it's not over yet. Tomorrow you get a chance to leave the last impression."

"But will it be a good one or another bad one?"

"That's up to you, Brick."

CHAPTER 13

A few minutes later, Jon turned onto his street and Neil proceeded towards his house, plodding along as fast as an octogenarian after double hip replacement surgery.

After walking one block the unexpected sound of two short, quick taps to a car horn instinctively turned Neil's head in its direction. Looking to his left, he saw his father's yellow AMC Pacer, covered by a winter's worth of muck and road salt and badly in need of a washing, pull to a sputtering stop alongside him at the curb.

"Want a lift?" Al asked with a smile, leaning over from behind the steering wheel and calling to his son through the partially rolled down passenger-side window. "Hop in."

Neil settled into the front seat as Al maneuvered the old clunker back onto the road.

"How was practice?" asked Al.

"We just scrimmaged," said Neil, grim faced and staring straight ahead.

"And...?"

"I was terrible. I struck out twice – and I looked bad doing it. I don't want to talk about it, okay?"

But Neil talked on anyway.

"I didn't make contact once – didn't even hit a foul ball," he continued in a frantic tone. "I think my swing's messed up. Can you pitch some balls to me at the field? We've got one more day of tryouts. I've got to fix this by tomorrow."

"Wait a minute," said Al. "Back up and tell me what happened from the beginning."

"Well, you know that kid from Woodbridge I told you and mom about? The guy from basketball tryouts? He's trying out for center field, but he's also a pitcher. He pitched against my team in today's scrimmage."

"Okay."

"His first pitch nearly took my head off."

"And then what?"

"Well…then he struck me out looking on a full-count curve. But…"

"So, he fooled you. So, what? That happens to major leaguers, too."

"Then, the next at-bat he drilled me right here with the first pitch."

Neil rolled up his left sweatshirt sleeve to reveal a black and blue welt tattooed on his bicep.

"He was purposely going after me," he continued. "I know it."

"How'd you react?" asked an impassive, seemingly oblivious Al, who didn't so much as peek at his son's ugly bruise.

152

"I struck out on three pitches my next time up," sighed Neil, now resigned to accepting that his father would not be offering the sympathetic ear he'd hoped to receive. "I was so mad that..."

"Well, *that's* the problem, right there. Your swing's not messed up. Your head's messed up. You can't hit when you're angry. That's not the right approach to take to an at-bat. You know that. I'll bet none of the pitches you swung at would have even been called strikes, would they?"

"Maybe one of them..."

"And you tried to kill the ball and swing for the fences, rather than just put it in play, right?"

Neil nodded in agreement.

"It sounds like you let that kid get inside your head and psych you out," Al continued. "You can't play baseball like that. Maybe some people can, but you can't, so don't try to play that game. Play *your* game. More batting practice isn't the answer. You could take a thousand extra cuts and they won't help you, if your head's not screwed on right. Remember what works for you. Tomorrow, concentrate on doing the things that have made you a good player.

"What happened to you in basketball was unfortunate, but you've done a great job rebounding from your mistakes. You learned from them. Physically, you've prepared yourself as well as you possibly could have – probably better than anyone there. Don't let that hard work go to waste. Channel your anger constructively. Forget about today. Don't let one bad day hurt you tomorrow, too. The past only exists in your head. It can't come back and hurt you again unless you let it, so forget it."

The taciturn Al made his point with all the emotion and passion of a keynote address delivered at an insurance underwriting seminar, but Neil received the message loud and clear. If he was going to shine in the next day's practice, then he had to shelve his anger, or else spill more tears over yet another lost opportunity.

~~~

For as long as Neil could remember, the weather tended to dictate his outlook and mood. While warm, sunny days seemed to give him strength, optimism and fill his adrenaline tank, by contrast, rainy or brutally cold days made him feel small, weak, and pessimistic.

The weather wasn't with Neil on the last day of tryouts. That afternoon, the temperature dropped to under forty five degrees and gray storm clouds hovered ominously.

If the temperature wasn't cold enough already, bone-chilling blasts of arctic air swept across the ball fields, as if to remind the players that spring would arrive only under Mother Nature's stubborn terms – and not from a set date on a calendar.

Dressed as warmly as he could without being too bulky and restrictive, Neil's long johns and sweatpants offered little protection against the March chill. Wind gusts swept through him like he was Swiss Cheese, pushing the dead leaves that had crept onto the field from the surrounding woods into the bottom of the chain link backstop, creating a haphazard tapestry of rust, brown and burnt orange colors.

His teeth chattering almost uncontrollably from both the cold and nervous energy, Neil did half jumping jacks between tosses with Jon during pre-practice warm ups. But every time he felt like he was getting loose, either the wind would whip in or a return throw from Jon would strike the palm of his glove rather than the webbing, stinging his hand with the intensity of a dozen bees.

Even the baseball – which for so long had seemed like a natural extension of Neil's right hand – felt foreign to him. The ball seemed heavy and he couldn't find a comfortable grip on it between his cold, stiff fingers. As Thorne had done the day before, the inclement weather started playing with Neil's mind and was now breaking down his body and game.

On the eve of cut-down day, Neil wasn't the only boy who seemed to be negatively affected by the pressure of the moment. No matter how confidently some of the players carried themselves, they all knew what was at stake, so everyone was on their best behavior. Next to the intermittent howling wind, the only sounds to be heard across the field during warm-ups was the irregular beat being played out by baseballs smacking into mitts.

After a few more minutes of playing catch, Preece called everyone together and announced the rosters for the day's scrimmages; once again, Neil and Jon were on the same team. After his inept performance the previous day, Neil fully expected to be dropped to the bottom of the batting order for the final scrimmage. But to his surprise, Neil again found himself batting leadoff.

Convinced that the student manager who'd announced the batting order was reading from yesterday's lineup card, would soon recognize his clerical error and put the right player in the first spot in the order, Neil quickly picked out a helmet, grabbed his bat and advanced towards the batter's box to start the game.

On the mound for the opposing team was a sophomore from Woodbridge, a left-hander, who Neil had faced a couple times in batting practice over the past ten days. Watching the pitcher throw his warm-up tosses, Neil recalled how, to date, he'd had a difficult time trying to hit the long, lanky boy's rising fastballs, which tended to ride in on his hands – preventing him from getting the barrel of the bat on the ball.

Neil scooped up a handful of dirt. Rubbing it vigorously into his bare hands, he thought how today of all days – with the cold temp and a pitcher on the mound who liked to jam right-handed hitters – it would be nice to own a pair of batting gloves. Choking up two inches on his bat, as usual, he took a deep breath, stepped into the batter's box, assumed his stance and recalled a piece of advice that Al shared with him that morning at the breakfast table: *First at-bat, take the first pitch – strike or not – so you break that overanxious rut you got yourself in to.*

Working from a full windup, the lefty delivered a low and inside fastball. Half way towards the ball's path to home plate, though, Neil dropped his father's plan. Sensing he might not see as good a pitch again that at-bat, he slid his hands up the barrel of his bat and dropped the head of it on the ball, steering it some twenty feet down the third baseline, where it died on the lip of the infield grass.

The bunt couldn't have been more perfectly placed than if Neil had set it there by hand. Neither the third baseman, who was playing even with the bag, nor the pitcher, with his momentum taking him towards the first base side of the plate, could make a play on it, and Neil easily beat the bunt out for a base hit.

Standing on first base, Neil took a deep breath and exhaled, releasing the pressure and tension he'd been collecting in his body for the past twenty four hours. Neil had made a heads-up play and it was a win-win all around. Not only had he gotten a hit, but Neil had done so without having to swing the bat and risk the potential pain associated with making contact with a ball on a cold day minus the cushioning benefit of batting gloves. Even more importantly, maybe he'd taken a step towards redeeming himself in Preece's eyes.

Working from the stretch position, the lefty pitcher took a cursory look at Neil, who had taken a three-step lead off first base. Apparently not thinking the lead long enough to warrant even his "B" move and a throw over to the bag, the sidewinder delivered to home plate. Compensating for his conservative lead, Neil got a great jump towards second base. Chugging as hard as he could, he slid to the outside corner of the bag, easily beating the catcher's throw to the shortstop, who'd run over to cover the base; the infielder never even bothering to apply a tag on Neil.

Brushing the hard dirt off his pants leg, Neil's energy level was now through the roof – despite the cold. *Settle down*, Neil said to himself, as he took his lead off second base. *That great bunt and stolen base will be wasted if I lose focus and get myself picked off.*

The count was 0 and 1 to the batter, Jon – his two hits in yesterday's scrimmage having earned him a seven-spot promotion in the batting order. Neil suspected that his lefty-hitting friend would probably not be able to pull the southpaw pitcher, so he took a relatively short lead off second base, wary that the second baseman, who was shading towards the middle of the infield, might sneak in behind him for a pickoff attempt.

Jon, indeed, swung late on the next two pitches, fouling them off weakly past third base. Taking another lead off second, Neil heard a familiar, grating voice behind him in center field.

157

"No stick, Kenny, no stick," bellowed Thorne. "Punch 'em out, man."

"No stick?!" an irritated Neil whispered to himself, turning his head toward center field. "That 'no stick' had two hits off you yesterday."

"Way to hang in there, Bisch," yelled Neil in encouragement to his friend at home plate. "You can do it…just like those meatballs you hit yesterday."

Neil took another short lead and peripherally watched for any movement from the second baseman or shortstop who might be slipping in behind him.

After throwing three consecutive fastballs, the pitcher finally went with his long, looping curve. Waiting on it perfectly, body weight transferring from his back foot to front foot, Jon swung and wrapped a hard grounder up the middle. With the ball hit to his left – behind him – Neil followed the fundamental base-running rules of the game and took off toward third base. Half way to the bag, he peeked over his left shoulder and saw the ball dribble into center field. Without breaking stride, Neil stepped on third base and headed for home just as the hard-charging Thorne picked the ball off the turf. Knowing the power behind Thorne's strong throwing arm, Neil reached deep to shift into a higher gear to complete the last leg of his trip around the bases.

Not wanting to turn his head even for an instant to track the ball and slow his stride, Neil kept his eyes straight ahead at the catcher, who had moved in front of the plate awaiting the throw from Thorne.

While the catcher's defensive position was a sign that maybe it wasn't going to be a bang-bang play at the plate, Neil wasn't about to take any chances. Without letting up, he slid feet first across the unblocked plate. Neil was safe and an instant later the ball passed several feet over his head, striking the backstop on the fly. Thorne, in trying to play the hero, had missed the cutoff man, allowing not only Neil to score but Jon to move into scoring position at second base.

A hit, a stolen base and aggressive base running capped off by a run scored...not a bad half inning, Neil thought as he took a seat in the dugout to wait out the rest of the frame. He wouldn't have minded if the sky suddenly opened up and rained a monsoon, ending the scrimmage right then and there and leaving Preece with that half inning as the snapshot for why he should be the freshman team's starting center fielder that season.

After two three-up-and-three-down half innings, Neil was in center field, with Thorne, the other team's cleanup hitter, leading off. By now the late-afternoon sun had begun to sink, causing the temperature to drop a few more degrees. The wind at Neil's back picked up, as well, to such an extent that the legs of his baggy sweatpants were fluttering madly like a flag on a pole in a gale. Neil was so cold that he'd resorted to plunging his bare hand down the front of his sweats between pitches in a desperate attempt to keep it warm.

With the weather conditions as they were, it would take quite a poke, Neil reasoned, for anyone – Thorne included – to reach the center field homerun fence. Moving in and to the left from the straightaway location he usually played, Neil removed his numbing hand and bent over in his defensive posture to await the first pitch. Connecting on the delivery, Thorne quickly sent the ball skyward, like a launched firecracker, towards left-center field.

159

Instinctively, Neil broke back, but as he did he noticed the strong wind had held up the ball. On a windless day, that ball would have carried to at least the warning track, but given the blustery conditions, nothing higher than a line drive stood much of a chance to travel very far. Retracing his steps, Neil caught the harmless fly at the spot from where he was originally positioned, some fifty feet from the infield. The bullheaded Thorne should have known better, Neil thought, than to swing for the fences on a day like today.

Neil's team was still leading 1-0 when he came to the plate in the top half of the third inning with no outs and a runner on second base. While a base hit and the prospect of going two for two at the plate, was appealing, Neil knew it would be gravy and that the situation called for him to sacrifice himself for the good of the team; to hit behind the runner and move him deeper into scoring position, where someone, ideally Jon, the next batter, could drive his teammate home. Even a little ground ball to the right side of the infield would get the job done.

For a moment, Neil considered bunting again, but thought better of it when he spotted the third baseman creeping onto the infield grass, preparing for a possible repeat attempt.

With his bunting strategy taken away, Neil moved onto Plan B. Choking up a half inch higher on the bat than normal for better control, Neil took his father's advice – albeit an at-bat late – and purposely let the first pitch go by for a called strike on the inside corner of the plate. He took the next pitch, as well, which was also on the inside corner of the plate, rather than swing and risk pulling it to the shortstop or third baseman, which would have kept his teammate moored at second base.

Behind 0 and 2 in the count now, Neil no longer had the luxury of taking strikes – or even borderline pitches. But being in the hole, he knew, was still no excuse for not moving the base runner to third. The coach would be less than impressed by a batted ball pulled to the left side or a comebacker to the mound.

"He's not swingin', Mikey, just lay it in there," Thorne yelled to the pitcher from his position in shallow center field. "No stick. No stick."

Annoyed by the putdown, Neil stepped out of the batter's box to take a deep breath and re-focus. Stepping back in, Neil set up a couple inches back off home plate, putting himself at risk for a ball on the outside corner that he couldn't reach. But, facing a pitcher who liked to bust right-handed hitters in on the fists, Neil figured it was a gamble worth taking. Up in the count, the lefty's next pitch came in low and outside. Even after adjusting for his new position at the plate, the pitch was too far outside for Neil's liking. Still, he held his breath until Preece called it a ball.

Maintaining his position, Neil stood in on the next pitch – a curve that normally would have broken inside. Now, however, it was the equivalent of a pitch that would have split the plate in half – had the base been moved three inches to the left. Using an inside-out-swing, Neil slapped at the ball and sent a slow chopper towards the second baseman. Running hard, Neil was thrown out at first by several feet, but the runner moved to third on the play. Mission accomplished. Taking a protracted look at Preece as he ran across the field to his team's dugout, Neil expected the ex-minor leaguer to acknowledge him for his baseball smarts and execution, but the stone-faced coach neither looked at nor said anything to him.

Neil's strategy bore fruit on the next pitch when Jon delivered a sacrifice fly to left field to give his team a 2-0 lead. An inning later, after the teams traded a pair of runs, the score was 3-1.

With one out and no one on base in the top of the fifth inning, Neil – his bare hands now practically ice to the touch – came up for what was likely to be his last at-bat of the game. Not wanting to risk getting jammed by an inside pitch and stinging them further, he jumped on the left hander's first pitch – a fastball on the outside corner of the plate, drilling it on a line between the first and second basemen into right field for a single.

Stranded at first base after the following two hitters popped out, Neil trotted out to center field for the bottom of the fifth inning, calculating his day's line score in his head. It read: 2 for 3 at the plate, with a run scored and a stolen base. And what wouldn't have shown up in a box score: His only out contributed to another of his team's runs. Not a bad game, he thought to himself. Contented and relaxed, Neil undid the zipper on his gray, hooded sweatshirt that had been fastened all the way up to his neck – the cold no longer bothering him as much.

A few minutes later came the capper to his day, Thorne striking out to end the game on a ball in the dirt and then repeatedly smashing his bat on the ground in anger, as if he was Pete Townshend laying waste to a guitar on stage.

"Good game, guys," said Preece addressing the huddled players shortly thereafter in the relative warmth of the third base dugout. "As a whole, I would have liked to see some more hitting today, but I think the weather had a lot to do with the quiet bats.

"Before we go, I want to say thanks to everyone for trying out. You all worked hard, so you should be proud of yourselves. Tonight, Coach Heliver and I will compare notes and decide who we think should be on the freshman and jayvee teams. The names of those who've made it will be posted on sheets outside our respective office doors at noon tomorrow. For those of you who make the teams, we'll be practicing at the usual time tomorrow afternoon."

Jon and Neil walked home that night happily replaying the game, feeling more confident and secure about their place on the freshman team. In Neil's mind he'd atoned for his previous day's abysmal performance and Jon, who picked up where he left off the day before with another hit, a sacrifice fly and two runs batted in, had been the most impressive hitter on either team.

That night, lying in bed, Neil stared at the darkness of his ceiling, a soft smile creasing his face. Somewhere behind the dark clouds that day, he felt like the stars had aligned for him. Neil hadn't succumbed to the pressures of tryouts – not the external ones, nor the internal demands he'd made on himself. Neil drifted off to sleep with his last thought being that he'd survived the cuts.

CHAPTER 14

Eight hours later, however, his outlook was much dimmer. Never a morning person, the confidence Neil had gone to sleep with had vanished from his bed by the time he'd awoke, like a sobered-up partner after a boozy, one-night stand.

Walking to school with Jon, Neil could only dwell on the mistakes he'd committed over the past two weeks and not what he'd accomplished. How he wasn't a power hitter or didn't possess a rifle throwing arm, like Thorne had. His paranoia running high, Neil imagined Preece providing the same scouting report to Heliver in their coaches' meeting and then recommending Neil not be added to the freshman team.

With all the neatness of a second grader writing in cursive for the first time, a shaky-handed Neil signed the attendance sheet in homeroom before going to the first of his four morning classes. Half a school day of waiting and worrying stood between him and the posting of the baseball teams' rosters.

Even under the best of circumstances, the four-hour interval between morning and lunch was like an endurance test to Neil. Unable to concentrate in class, the only "notes" he took that morning were to compulsively chart and evaluate the strengths and weaknesses of the other freshmen outfielders. As he long ago figured, the team was likely to carry only about half of the ten outfielders who tried out. And the way the increasingly fearful Neil interpreted his mock scouting report, he had only a fifty-fifty chance of making the team – never mind beating out Thorne for the starting center fielder's job.

Finally, at noon, Neil bolted from his desk located in the back of his American History class. Out of the classroom before the bell stopped ringing, he hurried to his locker to wait for Jon, so they could check out the freshman roster together.

"Where were you, man?" demanded an agitated Neil. "Class ended five minutes ago!"

"I wanted to talk to Mr. Raker about my English test next Tuesday," answered Jon, rotating the disk on his combination lock.

"Why couldn't that wait until Monday?

"Because, I wanted to get started on it this weekend. Will you relax already? The rosters aren't going anywhere."

The boys proceeded to make their way through the crowded hallways to the other side of school. Turning down the wing outside the gym, they saw three clusters of baseball hopefuls. Closest to them were juniors and seniors gathered outside the varsity coach's door. In the middle stood the aspiring junior varsity candidates, followed at the far end by Jon and Neil's freshmen classmates, crowding around Heliver's door.

Weaving through the masses, the boys made their way to Heliver's office. Peering over the shoulder of the boy in front of him, Neil began scanning the list. His heart racing faster with each passing second, he spotted Thorne's name on the top, followed by a couple kids he knew from Eastham Elementary, and then some unfamiliar names from Woodbridge. In the middle of the page he saw Jon's name. Only a half dozen or so more kids had to be left. Continuing to read, Neil passed a few more names of boys he knew and more of those he didn't. And then the list ended, without Neil's name being included.

No, not again, Neil thought. *This can't be right.* Convincing himself that in his excited state he must have somehow glossed over his own name, Neil began combing through the list again – this time, with the concentration of a professional proofreader. But once he passed Jon's name the second time through, Neil had a gut feeling his name wouldn't be found, no matter how hard he looked.

Turning away from the door, Neil's pastel-colored face began to drain of what little color remained in it. Not making the basketball team was a devastating blow to him at first, but Neil had come to terms with it when he understood he was neither good enough nor had done the prep work necessary to warrant a spot on the roster. But baseball was a different story.

In the crowded hallway, yet alone with his thoughts, Neil wondered what had gone wrong this time. All those solitary hours spent running, lifting and swinging a bat had apparently been for naught. If sacrifice and work were supposed to be rewarded, then why couldn't he cash the paycheck for his two months of hard labor?

Most of the boys who were left lingering in the corridor had made the team, including Thorne, who was laughing loudly with a few friends. Neil purposely avoided looking at him, worried that he might lose control and do something he'd later regret. All Neil wanted to do now was get out of the suddenly claustrophobic corridor as quickly as possible. He'd deal with his emotions later in private, like he always did. Already, Neil was making a return date with his drum set. Only this time, he'd make his post-basketball tryout encounter with the kit look like he was playing at a senior citizen's dance.

Turning around to leave, Neil and Jon started walking back up the hallway towards a large group of sophomores, who were still loitering at Preece's door.

"Hey, Neil, way to go, man!" said Dave Cavenall, the older boy he knew from Eastham Elementary, when the pair reached the door. "That's awesome!"

"Way to go, *what?*" answered Neil in disgust, lifting his head to lock eyes with the sophomore.

"Look."

Through squinting eyes, Neil followed Dave's pointed index finger to the jayvee team's roster taped to the coach's door. Almost immediately he spotted it. But because it seemed so out of context to him, a second or two went by before Neil fully grasped what Dave wanted him to see. Continuing to peer through the fog in his brain, the name slowly began to come into focus: *Neal Bricker (freshman)*.

"Brick, you did it!" cried an excited Jon. "You're on the jayvee!"

Not in Neil's wildest dreams did he consider the possibility of making the jayvee team as a freshman. All he'd aspired to was a spot on the freshman team. Any spot – backup or starter – would do. Yet, there was Neil's name, spelled incorrectly, but unmistakably his. Scrawled on a torn sheet of yellow notebook paper, it looked better than if it was up in lights on the Shea Stadium scoreboard. Neil had not only beaten Thorne out but he'd jumped a team ahead of him.

Nearly in shock, unable to speak and unaccustomed to being the focus of attention anyway, the only external emotion Neil could muster was a shy, pursed smile. Internally, though, Neil was having a party in his heart and head, his moment of raw joy made all the more intense and wondrous because of the failure he endured and hardships he'd overcome the past several months. It was the kind of satisfaction known only to those who had also experienced profound despair.

Jon's response, as well as those from some of the sophomores in the hallway aroused the curiosity of the freshman team, who moved over from Heliver's door to see what the commotion was about. Save for Thorne, most of them seemed genuinely happy when they learned of Neil's good fortune.

"What the hell?" Thorne said in disbelief, as he elbowed his way to the door to get a closer look at the list. "That's gotta be a mistake. No other freshman is even on the list. I'd check with Preece, if I were you, man, before showing up for jayvee practice. You wouldn't want to look stupid. I'd bet you're on the wrong list."

~~~

By now, Neil knew better than to think Thorne had his best interests in mind. Even though Preece had misspelled Neil's forename, the coach was too smart to make a mistake of the proportions that Thorne was suggesting. Still, Neil's rival had given him pause to question if his place on the jayvee team was worth confirming with the coach.

"You think maybe I should talk to Preece, just to be sure?" Neil asked Jon, when the two were alone at their lockers minutes later to retrieve their lunch bags.

"Awww, you know Thorne," said Jon. "That jerk's just tryin' to screw with you because he's jealous you made it to jayvee and he didn't. C'mon, let's go to lunch."

"Maybe, but it couldn't hurt to check."

"Well, don't try to talk to Preece now. Go after lunch. The list was just posted. Preece may not even be there and if he is he's going to think anybody who's knocking on his door is there to bitch about not making the team, so he probably won't even answer."

"Right. And if anybody *is* talking to him now it's probably Thorne complaining that he should have made jayvee and not me."

Returning to the athletic wing an hour later after being excused from study hall, Neil found Preece alone in his office.

"Hi, coach. Can I... talk with you for a minute?" asked Neil hesitantly, from the open doorway.

"What's on your mind, Neil?" asked Preece, motioning the boy into the room towards a seat across from his desk, before folding his hands in front of him.

"Well, I just wanted to see for sure if...umm..."

"Yes, Neil, you're really on the jayvee team."

"Yeah, that's what I wanted to know."

"I'm glad you stopped by. I wanted to talk with you about it. Sorry about how you found out. I wasn't thinking this through. That's what happens when I don't have a second cup of coffee in the morning. It didn't occur to me until later that you'd have no

169

reason to check the jayvee list and you would have assumed – and rightly so – that you were cut when you didn't see your name on the freshman roster.

"I also wanted to discuss how this is going to work. You're my starting center fielder and you're going to bat leadoff. I didn't bring you up to jayvee to sit on the bench. That wouldn't do you any good. Coach Heliver and I also worked out an arrangement where you'll go down and play on the freshman team and start in center whenever Bobby Thorne is scheduled to pitch and the jayvee doesn't have a game. You'll also go down and play with them whenever there's not a conflict with the two teams' schedules. You're going to get to play *a lot* of baseball this season. Sound good?"

"Yeah, *great*. Thanks, coach. I won't let you down."

"I know it's a little bit unusual for a freshman to jump right to jayvee, but I know you can handle it. I wouldn't have promoted you to jayvee, if I didn't think you could do the job. And don't thank me. You earned it. You played too hard not to make this team. You *stood* out, Neil."

Preece paused, as if to allow Neil time to run under the sentence like it was a fly ball and catch its meaning. Neil acknowledged the comment with a knowing nod and a shy smile before training his eyes on the floor. Neil had never forgotten the phrase "you didn't stand out," that Preece used to tell him why he hadn't made the basketball team. Apparently, Preece still remembered their previous conversation, too.

"I'm glad I could tell you that this time," Preece continued, extending his right hand.

170

"Me, too," said Neil, meeting it with his in a firm handshake, while looking his coach in the eye.

~~~

The reality of making the jayvee team didn't hit home for Neil until that afternoon's batting practice. Standing alone in the middle of the outfield during fielding drills for the first time since tryouts began, Neil finally had the position all to himself and no isolation ever felt more peaceful or secure. No longer would he be forced to share center field with the openly hostile Thorne – now safely tucked out of harm's way on a separate ball field where the freshman team was practicing – nor the freshman team's incumbent center fielder, a sophomore, who was cut from the jayvee squad to make room for Neil.

With none of the batters that chilly afternoon seemingly capable of lifting the ball out of the infield, Neil had plenty of time to daydream and soak in his accomplishment. Eventually, Neil's thoughts drifted back to seventh period English Literature and that afternoon's discussion of F. Scott Fitzgerald's *The Great Gatsby*. A paraphrased paragraph from the closing passage of the book suddenly popped into Neil's head.

...I thought of Gatsby's wonder when he first picked out the green light at the end of Daisy's dock. He had come a long way to this blue lawn and his dream must have seemed so close that he could hardly fail to grasp it. He did not know that it was already behind him...

Standing in the middle of his version of a blue lawn, Neil drew a parallel between himself and Gatsby, the enigmatic, self-made millionaire. For the past few months Neil had doggedly chased baseball the way Gatsby obsessively pursued his lost love, Daisy.

171

Like Gatsby, who built his fortune solely to impress Daisy, Neil drove himself to train so he could impress a baseball coach. But unlike Gatsby, whose dream was in his wake, Neil had much to look forward to and the only thing behind him was Thorne – figuratively and literally – toiling on the adjoining field. Through equal parts talent, preparation and force of will – Neil had overcome all challenges and challengers and reached his own green light. He wasn't about to let it slip through the fingers of his mitt.

When practice ended, Neil couldn't wait to get home to share his good news with his family. Finally secure enough with his place on the team to move into the players' locker room from his dressing room in the boys' restroom, Neil quickly crammed his flannel shirt, corduroys and Pumas into his gym bag, so as not to waste precious minutes changing. Convincing Jon to do likewise, the two power walked in their soiled sweatpants and sweatshirts to Jon's turnoff street, with Neil sprinting the rest of the way home.

Bursting through the back door of his house, Neil encountered Ann in the kitchen, her hands immersed in a bowl of uncooked ground beef.

"Good God, Neil!" exclaimed his mother. "You scared me half to death. Did somebody chase you home or something?"

"Where's dad?" a near-breathless Neil asked, setting his book and gym bags on a chair.

"He's in the parlor. Why? What's wrong?"

"Nothing. I just wanted to tell you…"

"Hey," said Al, emerging from the doorway separating the hallway and the kitchen and setting his empty coffee mug in the cradle of the Mr. Coffee machine on the counter. "Let me guess, you made the freshman team."

"Uh…why would you say that?" asked Neil.

"Because this is about the time you've been coming home the past two weeks. If you hadn't made the team, you'd have been home earlier, right?"

"Right…but, I didn't make the freshman team."

"You're kidding," said Al, his jaw dropping to his chin.

"Oh, honey, but you worked so hard," uttered his mother in disappointment. "I can't believe…"

"I made the jayvee team!" exclaimed Neil, breaking into a wide grin.

"All *right!*" shouted Al seconds later, after the news sunk in.

"Oh, that's wonderful, Neil," said Ann, grabbing her son in a stiff, forearm hug, so as not to touch his back with her raw-meat-soiled hands.

"The coach also told me I'm the starting center fielder and leadoff hitter," Neil announced proudly.

"Wow!" exclaimed Al. "Starting center fielder as a freshman on jayvee…you must have *really* impressed that coach. I think we should celebrate. How about pizza tonight?"

"Al, can't you see I'm up to my elbows in ground beef here?" remarked an incredulous Ann. "We're having meatloaf, remember?"

The commotion in the kitchen attracted the attention of Molly and Gerry, who came running from various points in the house.

"What's going on?" asked Molly.

"Your brother made the jayvee baseball team," said a beaming Al, draping an arm around Neil's shoulders. "Let's put this to a vote. Would you kids like pizza for dinner or meatloaf?"

"Pizza, pizza!" shouted Gerry, jumping up and down.

"Why pizza?" asked Molly. "I thought we were having meatloaf."

"That was my assumption, too, but I just work here apparently," sighed Ann.

"Pizza, pizza," slowly repeated Gerry in a monotone, as if in a trance.

"Okay, pizza it is then. I'll order a couple of pies from Sal's," declared Al, reaching for the rotary dial telephone mounted on the kitchen wall to call a number he knew by heart as if it was his own.

"Fine," said a resigned Ann. "Who am I to stand in the way of pizza?"

"Ann, by the time the meatloaf's cooked, we'd be well into our first pie," said Al, covering the mouthpiece of the phone with his hand, while he waited for Sal's to answer. "We can have the meatloaf tomorrow. And since this is such a special occasion, let's eat in the dining room."

"Pizza, in the dining room?!" said his wife, with a "what's next?" look.

"Why not? What are we saving it for?" replied Al. "We haven't eaten in there since Christmas dinner."

A half an hour later the Brickers began gorging themselves on plain cheese and pepperoni pies on china that had previously only been reserved for holiday dinners, and washing them down with plastic cups of Orange Crush soda.

"I don't want to spoil the festive mood, but we got some bad news today," Ann somberly announced to the family. "Your uncle George died."

"Who?" asked Molly, peeling a piece of pepperoni off her slice of pizza and dropping it into Gerry's mouth, as if the boy was a trained seal.

"Molly Catherine! Gerald Anthony!" exclaimed Ann, "Is that appropriate table manners?"

"Uncle George from Rhinebeck," answered Al. "You met him at the family reunion last summer."

"Oh...*that* Uncle George," replied Molly. "Isn't he the one who wore black dress socks with shorts? But he's not really our uncle. He was your uncle, mom. We didn't really know him."

"He was still your relation," Ann said.

"Did he have a family?" asked Gerry, reaching into the open pizza box in the middle of the table to remove another slice with pepperoni.

"He was married to your Aunt Jean," said Ann. "She was his third wife."

"Three times married…unreal," said Al, shaking his head in disbelief. "Everyone's entitled to a marriage mulligan, but *three* times?! Wasn't the last one his mistress while he was married to his second wife? It's hard to believe there was even *one* woman interested in an alcoholic bigot, who collected unemployment checks for half his life. He's the only person I've ever met who actually got mad when he played the lottery and didn't win. He acted like the odds were in his favor. They'll probably bury him in a scotch bottle."

"Al, enough!" shot back Ann pointedly. "It's a good thing you're not giving the eulogy."

"Mommy, what's a mistress?" asked Gerry.

"This isn't exactly proper dinner-table conversation, but since your father brought it up, maybe he should answer that question," Ann said, looking sternly at her husband.

"A mistress is a woman, who is…ahhh…*friendly*, you could say, with a married man," answered Al, measuring his words carefully. "It's a bit complicated to explain, Ger. When you're older you'll understand."

"Why do I always have to wait until I'm older to find out things? Daddy, do you have a mistress?" inquired Gerry innocently, as the rest of the table burst into laughter.

176

"No," exclaimed Al, choking back a spit take from his swig of soda. "It's not a good thing for a married man to have a mistress. Besides, I don't have the time to have a mistress. It's too much work as it is just to have a wife."

"Very funny, Al," said a bemused Ann, picking up a piece of pizza crust from her plate and faking as if she'd hurl it across the table at her husband.

"Ah, mom, is that good table manners?" asked Molly in a mock scold.

"What'd Uncle George die of," inquired a persistent Gerry, who asked more questions in an average day than Socrates posed in a month.

"Cancer," replied Ann.

"I'm surprised," deadpanned Neil. "He looked healthy enough to me when I saw him at the reunion smoking a cigarette."

"Okay, stop with the jokes," said Ann. "You should all be more respectful."

"Your mother's right, kids," said a serious-looking Al. "To honor him, I'll wear my dress socks at half staff – or make that half calf – tomorrow."

Neil, Molly and Marc, old enough to understand the reference, laughed without hesitation. After a slight pause, Gerry joined in, wanting to be part of the joke even if he didn't have a clue why it was so funny to the others.

"Well, I'm going to the funeral on Tuesday, if anyone wants to join me," said Ann.

"I have a math test that day," replied Molly.

"Me, too," chipped in Marc.

"I hope I have one," quipped Neil.

"Yeah, honey, they're really broken up about it," said Al, stripping another wedge from the cheese pie.

"How've you been doing in math this semester, Molly?" asked Ann, finally throwing up a white flag on the previous subject.

"Okay, I guess," her daughter replied. "Well, good enough that my teacher asked me to tutor a kid in my class at recess this week."

"Who's that?" asked Marc.

"Bobby Thorne," his sister replied.

Across the table, Neil, working on his fifth slice of pizza of the meal, almost began to gag.

"What are you wasting your time with that jerk for?" asked Neil, after he'd cleared his throat.

"Neil, watch your language!" scolded his mother.

"What's wrong with Bobby?" asked Molly. "All the other boys in that class are so obnoxious...always asking me out on dates. He doesn't do that. He's a really nice guy."

"To cheerleaders maybe," huffed Neil.

"Is that the boy from basketball that you had a problem with, Neil?" asked Ann.

"Yeah," said Neil. "Just be careful around him, Moll."

"Oh, I'm really worried about him when we're doing algebra in the library," said Molly sarcastically, adjusting the spaghetti-strap on the left shoulder of her Tube top.

"Suit yourself," replied Neil. "It's your funeral. I'm just saying, I wouldn't trust that guy."

CHAPTER 15

Neil and his jayvee teammates spent the next two weeks preparing for the early April season opener. While he already knew the sophomores from Eastham – if only on a casual basis – having grown up and attended elementary school with them, his teammates from Woodbridge were complete strangers to him.

Initially, his Woodbridge teammates gave Neil the cold shoulder, as it'd been one of their own who'd been cut to make room for him on the jayvee roster. But soon enough, they noticed the same qualities in his game that had caught Preece's attention. Every time Neil out ran them all in sprint drills, tracked down a sure extra base hit in center field or displayed his savant-like ability to put the ball in play nearly every time he swung a bat, his older teammates realized that Neil could more than hold his own with them at the jayvee level. "Rookie," as they affectionately nicknamed the shy teen, became impossible to resent, if not possible to get close to.

Four days before the season opener, both the freshman and jayvee teams got their first weekday off since practice began. Naturally, Neil and Jon spent their free day glued to the TV at Neil's house, watching the New York Mets' season opener that afternoon after school on WWOR, Channel 9.

Even old Shea Stadium, the Mets' home ballpark, dressed up for the occasion, sporting a new coat of blue paint on its façade and a ghastly, gauche yellow on its seats – four fifths of which were empty due to a citywide transit strike and general fan apathy.

By the ninth inning of the Mets' eventual 5-2 win over the Cubs, Shea already looked in mid-season form. In the dim, late-afternoon sun, the stadium's off-season spruce job looked like it had worn off faster than a $1.99 makeover, reducing Shea to its usual cold, drab self. Jet planes landing at and taking off from nearby LaGuardia Airport buzzed overhead, while hotdog wrappers swirled about like snowflakes in a shaken snow globe, seemingly outnumbering what was left of the announced crowd of 12,219 fans.

"Do you think the Mets have that stupid mule again this year?" asked Jon, referring to the team mascot, Mettle the Mule, which often roamed the upper deck of the stadium during games.

"I can't believe they'd still have that thing," sighed Neil, digging his hand into a can of generic brand potato sticks. "It's so lame."

"I saw a Mets game last year and the camera showed the mule taking a dump on a seat."

"Cut it out. That never happened."

"No, I swear it's true. Murphy and Kiner were joking about it. I think it was in the mezzarine section."

"Mezzarine?! It's mezza*nine*."

Turning their attention back to the game itself, the Cubs were now down to their last two outs and Mets relief pitcher Neil Allen was facing Cubs pinch hitter Scot Thompson with a runner on first base.

"The Mets have yet to turn a double play in today's game, but now would be an opportune time for one," said Mets TV play-by-play man Bob Murphy. *"Last year, New York's pitchers led the National League in double plays turned, with an average of almost one per ballgame."*

181

"I'm not sure I'd brag about that stat," said Neil cynically, climbing out of his beanbag chair to fiddle with the UHF antenna on the TV. "The only reason they probably did was because their pitchers were always putting guys on base."

"Cut 'em some slack," said Jon. "It's good for the Mets to lead the league in something besides losses, for a change."

"Allen works from the stretch and looks into Stearns for the sign," continued Murphy. *"He shakes off one...now, he's ready...and here's the pitch...Thompson hits a bouncer to third, gloved by Maddox. He goes to Flynn at second for one...and across to Mazzilli for two. A 5-4-3 double play and the Mets win the gaaaame. The Mets take the 1980 Season Opener – the first win of the Wilpon-Doubleday ownership group – by the score of 5 to 2!"*

"Get those playoff tickets printed," Jon joked. "The Mets are in first place and unbeaten."

"Better enjoy it while it lasts," said Neil.

"Starting pitcher Craig Swan earns the win, Neil Allen the save, and the Cubs' Rick Reuschel takes the loss," Murphy continued. *"We'll be back... with the happy recap... after this word from Manufacturers Hanover."*

"A word from Manufacturers *Hangover*," cracked Jon, in his best Murphy imitation, before popping a handful of dry Quisp cereal into his mouth.

"What do you know about hangovers?" demanded Neil, laughing. "The only time you've ever had booze has been when you get the wine at Eucharist in church."

"Yeah, like you can talk. You've never been drunk before, either."

"Wanna stay and watch *Kiner's Korner?*" asked Neil, referring to the Mets' post-game TV show, hosted by Hall of Fame player and Mets announcer Ralph Kiner. "That's always good for a laugh."

"Did you say Kiner's coroner?" answered Jon.

"Cut it out."

"Hey, speaking of drunk, I think Thorne was drunk at practice yesterday?"

"Bull crap. On a school day?"

"Well, he was definitely on something. He's been acting really weird in practice lately."

"What's Heliver do about it? Anything?"

"No. You know Thorne can get away with murder at that school. He was talking about you during warm-ups yesterday."

"What'd he say?"

"He wanted to bet some guys that you won't last more than three games at jayvee and then you'll be sent down to freshman and sit behind him."

"What a jerk! The coach told me I'll only be playing freshman when the jayvee schedule allows. The only time I'll be playing behind him is when I'm in center and he's pitching."

"Don't worry. I stuck up for you."

"What'd you say?"

"I told him you'd at least make it to six games before you got demoted."

"Thanks for nothing."

"Hey, Marc-o," greeted Jon, as Neil's brother entered the rec room. "How's it hanging?"

"What's up?" said Marc curtly, stopping to retrieve his Aerosmith record that was lying near the family stereo before turning to take it from the room.

"What's *his* problem?" Jon asked Neil, after Marc had ascended the basement steps. "He still holding a grudge against me for narcing on him to you about what he was doing at Thorne's party?"

"Guess so. Join the club. I don't think he's too happy with me, either," said Neil. "That was more words than he's said to me in weeks."

"I don't get it. You said you didn't rat him out to your folks, right? You kept a lid on it."

"Oh, yeah, a real air-tight lid on it."

~~~

At the following day's practice, Neil, still angered over Thorne's remarks about him, pointedly stole glances up the small crest at the field where the freshman team was working out. Seeking inspiration from the uninspired, Neil combed through the knots of skinny teens, before locating the strapping Thorne.

"Gotta keep working hard," Neil whispered to himself. "No way I'm gonna be Thorne's caddy on the freshman team."

Every time he looked up and saw Thorne laugh, Neil imagined it was he who was the butt of the joke. The more his unwitting muse snickered, the faster Neil ran that day, the harder he concentrated and the more determined he was to excel.

Thorne would only be present in spirit when the season opened three days later. While the East Hill freshmen played at Brockton Park High School, the jayvee squad hosted their counterparts from the non-conference school located in a cramped, hardscrabble town in the heart of southeastern Bergen County.

After over a month of practice, Neil was more than ready to play in a real game, even if he didn't look the part. Despite picking the smallest size available, Neil was practically swimming in his pup tent of a uniform. Two sets of legs could have fit in the pants and the sleeves on his jersey extended well past his elbows. Even the cup in his athletic department issued jock strap offered more than enough room to roam.

"East Hill must be in rough shape this year," mumbled the Brockton Park catcher through his mask, when Neil came to the plate in the bottom of the first inning. "The bat boy's playing… and he's hittin' leadoff, too."

Flushed with confidence on the heels of making a running shoestring catch of a line drive to end the top of the inning, Neil ignored the cheap crack and dug vigorously at the batter's box dirt with the spikes of his right cleat. Now setting his feet in the box,

Neil looked out to the mound at the broad-shouldered, lightly mustachioed starting pitcher – just one of a dozen or so kids from Brockton Park that Neil observed during pregame warm-ups, who looked like he'd entered puberty during Richard Nixon's aborted second term in office. *As bad as East Hill is, I'm glad I don't go to Brockton*, Neil thought at the time. *I wouldn't make it through the Pledge of Allegiance at that school.*

"You look kinda scared, kid," said the catcher, briefly raising his mask before spitting on the ground near Neil's cleats. "Nervous, or something? Want us to pitch underhand to you?"

Neil continued to disregard the catcher's words.

"That's enough, son," said the home plate umpire to the catcher. "Knock off the chit-chat and just play the game. You ready, batter?"

"Yeah," Neil said, still looking towards the mound.

"Okay. Play ball!" yelled the ump, jabbing his right hand index finger at the Brockton Park pitcher.

Picking up his sign from the catcher the pitcher went into his windup. Coming straight over the top, the right hander delivered a fastball belt high over the heart of the plate. Defying the unofficial rule requiring a leadoff batter to at least take the first pitch, Neil swung and connected, sending a hard ground ball past the pitcher and through the infield for a clean base hit.

Rounding first base, he went a fourth of the way to second before retreating to the bag when the center fielder gathered in the ball and returned it to the infield. His heart beating so hard with excitement that it seemed like only his buttoned-up uniform jersey was keeping it from jumping from his chest, Neil delivered a hard low five to the upturned palm of a teammate, who was coaching first base.

"Nice hit, rookie," said the youth. "Thatta way to start us off. Don't forget to look at Preece for a signal."

Neil stared over to the coaching lines at third base. Raising his left hand over his forehead, in part to block the glare from the sun as much as to shield his view from Ann and Gerry, who were applauding and yelling loudly in the bleachers just over the coach's shoulder, Neil looked for his sign.

Touching the bill of his cap, Preece began cycling through a series of movements. Over the next ten seconds, the coach randomly tapped or tugged on various parts of his uniform and face. During one particular sequence, Neil held back a chuckle after Preece made the sign of the cross. Finally, the coach touched each cheek and clapped his hands twice.

"Got it?" the first base coach asked Neil.

Neil nodded, but by the time Preece had finished running through the complex series of signals, he wasn't sure whether his assignment was to steal second base on the next pitch or say grace.

Taking a four-step lead, Neil felt confident that he could get a good jump on the pitcher. As it was early in the game, the hard clay on the base path had yet to be chewed up by runners and would likely provide good traction. Plus, he wasn't nearly as worried about the pickoff move of a right-handed pitcher as he was a lefty, who didn't have to turn his whole body to throw to first base.

With a runner on base, the Brockton Park right hander went to his stretch position on the mound. Before beginning his windup, the pitcher gave a casual – but purposeful – look over his left shoulder, as if an intimidating stare would be enough to scare Neil from straying too far off the bag.

Following the pitcher's motion, Neil made sure the right hander was delivering to home plate before he pivoted his body and bolted towards second base, sliding feet first and making it safely without even drawing a throw from the catcher.

Brushing the caked-on dirt from his pant legs, Neil again checked with Preece for a sign. Nothing was on for the next pitch – or during the several that followed – as the Brockton Park pitcher mowed East Hills' numbers two and three hitters down on strikes. With two outs in the inning, the cleanup hitter, first baseman Steve Trelewitz, worked the count full.

"Neil…two outs. You go on the crack of the bat, okay?" reminded Preece, calling out to him through cupped hands.

Nodding in agreement, Neil took his lead off second base. Getting his bat head in front of the plate, the left-handed hitting Trelewitz pulled the next pitch on the ground toward the hole between first and second base. Neil pushed for third and looked up to see Preece vigorously wind milling him home with his right arm. Stepping on the bag and taking a wide turn, Neil stole a glance to his left in time to catch the Brockton Park right fielder pick up the ball and line up a throw to home plate.

Turning his focus back to the base path, Neil saw the catcher positioning himself on the third base side of the plate. If Neil was going to score, it appeared that he'd have to go through the hulking catcher to do so – and sliding feet or headfirst wouldn't get the job done. Neil would have to bowl him over. For someone who spent his life trying to stay away from head-on collisions, the one looming in front of Neil looked to be unavoidable.

Maybe, Neil said to himself as he ran, *the throw won't be in time or will be off line and the catcher will have to move out of the way to field it*. But the throw was true and the catcher stood his ground. Neil had no choice now but to hurtle his 120-pound frame into his opponent and hope to emerge in one piece; scoring the run would be icing on the cake.

Five feet from home plate, Neil lowered his left shoulder, shut his eyes and braced for the inevitable collision. Half a second later, the receiver caught the right fielder's throw. Wheeling to his left, he forcefully thrust his arms up into Neil's body to apply the tag, as if delivering a block in football. Neil struck the catcher full on, but despite all the momentum from a full head of steam, the smaller youth got the worst of the play – the catcher's block tag standing the runner upright, then knocking him backwards.

The impact of the collision, however, had been enough to jar the ball loose from the catcher's mitt. Now, both the ball and Neil were on the ground – no more than a foot away from home plate. The umpire, who had begun to raise his arm to call Neil out, lowered it and took two steps towards the plate to get a better vantage point for the developing play. Momentarily dazed from the collision – but aware enough to know that he hadn't touched home plate yet – Neil lunged forward from his seated position, just as the catcher barehanded the ball, slapping his hand hard on the plate a split second before he was tagged on the back.

"Safe!" shouted the ump, spreading his arms wide.

Pulled to his feet and bear hugged in congratulations by East Hills' on-deck batter, Neil – adrenaline coursing through every gland in his body – briefly stepped out of character.

"Not bad for a bat boy, huh?" Neil muttered softly to the catcher, the knob on his courage meter locked in at "one," making him incapable of voicing a louder response.

Two innings later – and after two more sparkling running catches in the outfield – Neil came up to bat again with East Hill still leading 1-0.

"Hey, the bat boy's back," greeted the catcher, his mouth curling into a wise guy smirk behind the bars on his facemask.

"The bat boy hit you pretty good," said Neil, still keyed up from their last meeting as he looked up to the hulking catcher.

"I've been hit harder by chicks."

"What'd I say the last time about talking?" said the umpire, taking off his mask and stepping between the two players. "Any more words from you guys and you're both out of the game. Understood?"

Neil set up deep in the batter's box and proceeded to take another half step back. Waiting for the first pitch, he warmed up by revolving his bat around once…twice…then on the third time extended his arms a few inches further, sending the barrel smack into the catcher's mask.

The force of the blow dropped the Brockton Park youth to his knees. His mask now laying in the dirt, the glassy-eyed catcher looked like he'd just been struck on the chin by a George Foreman right hand that was holding the heavy weight boxer's yet-to-be-invented grill.

"Sorry, man. Are you okay?" Neil innocently, but insincerely, asked the catcher.

Rushing to the woozy catcher's side, the home plate umpire and the Brockton Park head coach examined the teen for signs of a concussion.

"Nice hit, Neil," said a smirking Dave Cavenall, East Hill's number two hitter, when Neil retreated to the on-deck circle to wait out the delay.

"That was an accident," fibbed Neil.

"Yeah, and I'm Bob Dylan. What do you think they're asking the kid?"

"Probably questions about his juvenile delinquent record."

Moments later, the umpire – satisfied that the knock to the catcher's face had done no apparent neurological damage – summoned Neil back to home plate.

With play resumed, the Brocton Park receiver now set up defensively half a foot deeper in the box. Once again, Neil went through the same exaggerated arm motion with his bat. And every time he brought it behind him, the wary catcher scooted back another inch.

With the Brockton Park pitcher on a roll, having struck out four of the previous five batters, Neil looked curve ball on the first pitch. Shaking off the catcher once, the pitcher nodded at the next sign and went into his motion. Neil never flinched as the pitch started out inside then broke sharply to the outside part of the plate. Without a strike on him – never mind two, which would have necessitated he protect the plate or risk striking out – Neil didn't have to swing at this pitcher's pitch. No doubt his father in the stands was thinking Neil should wait for *his* pitch. But this *was* Neil's pitch because he had a good hunch it was coming. Stepping towards the ball, Neil reached out and slapped a line drive over the leaping second baseman's outstretched glove into right field for a base hit. Two pitches: Two hits. Neil had been in the batter's box that day for as long as he'd want to spend in a burning building.

Neil was only slightly more patient in his third and final at-bat of the game, taking two pitches before getting his third hit of the game – a line drive up the middle – before the now-mute catcher.

By game's end Neil had accounted for half of his team's hits and scored its only run – a marker that proved to be the difference in East Hill's season-opening win and a victory that he appropriately enough capped off with a sliding catch in center field. Popping to his feet after the grab, Neil floated as if on Cloud Nine toward his team's dugout and then quickly through the post-game handshake line.

After slapping the last opposing player's hand, Neil looked for his parents, who were slowly sidestepping their way off the bleachers – following Gerry, hopping like a frog down the metal grandstand. Catching eyes with his father, Al gestured towards the parking lot. Neil nodded and after changing into his street clothes in the locker room, met his family at their car.

CHAPTER 16

"So, why'd you swing at the first pitch in two of your at-bats?" asked Al from the driver's seat, before Neil had even slid shut the back door of the VW bus. "I thought leadoff batters were supposed to take pitches and work the count."

"Al, say something nice, for crying out loud!" cried Ann, smacking her husband across the shoulder with the back of her hand and turning around to face the backseat. "Don't listen to your father, Neil. *You* played great."

"Yes, you did," replied Al, smiling crookedly and winking into the rearview mirror at Neil, as he turned the key in the ignition. "You played very well. But, you could still afford to be a little more patient at the plate. I think you'd score points with your coach if you were."

"You mean more points than going three for three at bat would?" said a grinning Neil.

That night, in the same notebook where months before he'd so meticulously drafted a workout regimen and then recorded his daily progress, Neil jotted down his stats for his debut jayvee game.

Writing more carefully and neatly than he would if he was penning a book report, Neil penciled in the numbers from his perfect day: At-bats: 3, runs: 1, hits: 3, runs batted in: 0, stolen bases: 1, putouts: 4. No matter what he accomplished the rest of the season, this would be his high-water mark. He'd proven in his first game to any lingering doubters – including himself – that he deserved his jayvee promotion. Neil's only regret was not being able to see Thorne's reaction when the bully got wind of the game that he'd played.

~~~

Neil played two more jayvee games that week, coming back to earth with forgettable efforts of 1 for 4 at the plate in one contest and 0 for 3 in another.

The following Saturday, he suited up for his first game for the freshman team, starting in center field while Thorne pitched. Even though Neil was glad to be on a team with his best friend, all things being equal, he'd have rather been curled up on the top of his warm bunk bed that morning rather than shivering through fielding practice in the wind tunnel that passed for Cedarville High's outfield.

Moments before East Hill took their turns at the plate in the top half of the first inning, Heliver motioned Neil to the corner of the dugout for a private conversation.

"Neil, I know you're been batting leadoff up at jayvee, but I wanted you to understand why I'm putting you ninth in the order today," said Heliver. "We have a pretty set lineup now, so I don't really want to upset it – especially, given that you'll only be an occasional loaner from jayvee."

"Oh…okay, coach," replied Neil politely. "Whatever you say."

"I knew you'd be good with it," said Heliver, flashing his toothy grin. "Plus, now we can have a leadoff man at the bottom of the order, too."

Heliver slapped Neil on the butt and walked away.

A leadoff man at the bottom of the order?! Neil thought. *Who's he crapping?*

Whatever Heliver's motivation for the move, it didn't really matter to Neil what number he was hitting in the order, because he didn't plan on swinging the bat that day. At breakfast that morning, Al suggested the freshman game would be a good opportunity for Neil to work on his bunting under game conditions, so it would be perfected for the more meaningful jayvee contests. Neil agreed, although with his team trailing 4-0 already by the time he got his first at-bat leading off in the top of the third, he was having second thoughts about whether he should go through with it or not. Batting the idea around in his mind while loosening up in the on-deck circle, Neil decided that swing away or bunt, it made no difference. His team needed to get men on base, so he might as well stick with the original game plan.

The Cedarville third baseman also knew East Hill needed base runners, so he played Neil in on the grass to take away a bunt attempt. Trying to drag a bunt to third against this defensive alignment would have resulted in a sure out, Neil figured, so he improvised. With the count one ball and no strikes, Neil bunted the next offering hard on the ground toward the right side of the mound – a push bunt that the left-handed pitcher had no chance to field. Neither did the second baseman, who was back on his heels and playing near the outfield grass. No play was made and Neil legged the bunt out for a hit. One batter and one out later Jon nailed a double into the gap in left-center field that plated Neil, who was running on contact.

In the bottom of the inning, Thorne, who'd been struggling all game with command of his pitches, gave the run back – plus three more. Watching it all unfold in front of him from center field –

Thorne's walks, wild pitches and temper tantrums – Neil couldn't help but silently root for the slaughter to continue. And if his team had to suffer in the process, well, so be it. That was just collateral damage.

A few weeks earlier, Neil learned the term *schadenfreude* in German class. At the time, the concept of taking pleasure in the misery of others seemed cruel and unfathomable to him. Now, watching Thorne taking his lumps on the mound in front of friends, family and dozens of spectators, *schadenfreude* made perfect sense to Neil.

Almost as enjoyable for Neil as witnessing Thorne's epic failure on the field, was watching the pitcher's father's reaction in the stands, yelling at his son for every mistake the youth made and questioning nearly every one of the home plate umpire's ball and strike calls. The scene made for great theater and Neil was now thankful that he wasn't sleeping in that morning after all.

Finally, with no outs, the bases full and East Hill trailing 8-1, Heliver waddled to the mound on his stick legs, conferred with Thorne and the catcher for a moment and then motioned back to the sidelines for the relief pitcher, who'd been warming up since the start of the inning.

"Boo," cried Neil, softly to himself. "C'mon, coach, leave him in. Give him a few more batters."

To Neil's great delight, however, the scene was just getting started. Despite clearly being off his game, Thorne arrogantly refused to give up the ball when the reliever came to the mound. Neil watched in detached bemusement as Thorne and Heliver exchanged what looked to be heated words. A minute later, the second act of the melodrama came to an end. Thorne reluctantly gave up the baseball and began to sprint toward center field like a charging bull.

"Go to left!" Thorne barked, when he got to within about twenty feet of Neil.

"What?" Neil asked, hearing what Thorne said, but not understanding.

"What are you, freakin' deaf? Go play left field! I'm playing center now. And when you get there tell Lowery the coach said he's benched."

Neil did as he was told and crossed the outfield to assume his new defensive position. Cedarville went on to score two more runs that inning, with Neil continuing to silently cheer for each run that crossed the plate, knowing full well that the inherited base runners counted against Thorne's ballooning earned run average.

Back on the bench after the last out of the inning was recorded, stat-freak Neil giddily calculated Thorne's numbers for the game in his head: two innings pitched and ten earned runs for a seven-inning game, translated to a bloated E.R.A. of 35.00.

Ten minutes later – after Thorne had struck out for the second time in the game on a ball in the dirt – Neil and his teammates took the field for the bottom of the fourth inning.

If Thorne had lost something off his fastball on the mound that day, Neil couldn't tell by his warm-up throws. What should have been a casual, between-innings exercise between the two neighboring outfielders instead became an exercise in self-defense for Neil. Red faced and wild eyed, Thorne displayed more accuracy now than he'd shown on the mound, hitting Neil's mitt extra hard with every throw, all the while lobbing verbal bombs.

"How can you play jayvee with an arm like that?" sneered Thorne, punctuating his question by catching one of Neil's lollipop throws with his bare hand.

Angered, Neil put more mustard on his next throw.

"That couldn't break a pane of glass," goaded Thorne, not satisfied with Neil's best effort yet. "There's chicks on the softball team with better arms than you. These throws couldn't hurt a fly."

Accepting the return toss, Neil narrowed his eyes and set his jaw.

"Let's see if this one is hard enough for you," said the beleaguered youth under his breath, gritting his teeth and firing the ball back.

Leaning back on his right foot for extra leverage, Neil followed through, unleashing a low line drive that bounced about five feet short of Thorne. Hopping up quickly like a flat rock skipped across the surface of a lake, the ball struck Thorne flush in the groin, an instant before the youth could drop his mitt down to catch it. Collapsing to his knees in agony, Thorne rolled over onto his stomach, clutching his crotch with both hands.

"Was that hard enough for you, Thorne?" Neil asked, talking quietly into his glove to conceal a Cheshire cat smile. "Think that would have broken a pane of glass? Try wearing a cup next time."

Still writhing on the ground in pain, Thorne attracted the attention of everyone in attendance.

"What happened to him?" asked Jon, sidling over to Neil from his position at third base, while Heliver, Mr. Thorne and the second base umpire attended to the stricken center fielder.

"My warm-up throw hit him in the balls," answered Neil, barely suppressing a laugh.

"Hey, that's a three pointer, Brick!" Jon cackled, recalling the game that he and the infielders played during tryouts where a student manager was used for target practice.

"It's gotta be worth more than that."

Returning to his position when Thorne had caught his breath and Heliver and Mr. Thorne had left the field, Neil marveled at his surprising accuracy. With the possible exception of cutting down a runner at the plate to end a game, Neil considered the errant toss the greatest he'd ever made – or would *ever* make.

Thorne received a metaphorical shot below the belt at game's end, when, after another disagreement with Heliver on the team bus home, he was indefinitely suspended from the team.

CHAPTER 17

Over the next ten days, Neil lived in a state of baseball bliss. On the jayvee team, he settled into being a consistent .280 to .290 hitter, its leading base stealer and a flawless outfielder, who caught whatever he ran down. And in the three games Neil played for the freshman club during that span, and in Thorne's absence, he was a hitting machine – consistently rapping out two and three-hit games against pitchers who threw slower fastballs and earlier-breaking curveballs than he was used to seeing at the jayvee level.

Neil's carefree life proved short-lived, however, with the announcement that Thorne's sentence had been lifted.

"I can't believe Thorne's suspension was for only three games," said an incredulous Neil, talking on the telephone to Jon early one Friday night in late April. "What a joke. If anyone else had gotten into two arguments like that with a coach, he'd have been kicked off the team for good."

"You shoulda seen it," laughed Jon, twirling his long phone cord like a jump rope. "We're dressing for practice and Heliver comes in the locker room with Thorne and tells everyone that the jerk's back on the team because his attitude has improved. Then, someone makes a joke about what the coach said and when Heliver's back's turned, Thorne says 'Fuck you' and punches the kid in the arm."

"Yeah, it sounds like his attitude has *really* improved. So, can you go to this party tonight, or what?"

"No can do. My aunt, uncle and cousins are driving up from Virginia *tonight* now, instead of tomorrow. They'll be here in an hour. I gotta stick around."

"Great. Now, this night's *really* gonna be a bummer."

"You don't *have* to go, you know. Nobody's forcing you."

"I don't wanna go, believe me. Thorne's house is the *last* place I wanna spend a Friday night at. But it's the first time all year Marc's asked me to do something, so I guess I should."

"You guys talking again?"

"Not really. I'm pretty sure this was all my mom's idea and she put him up to it. She was acting like she knew ahead of time when I told her where we were going."

"You didn't tell her you were going to a party, did you?"

"C'mon, I'm not *that* stupid. She thinks we're going to the movies?"

"How're you getting there?"

"Some junior Marc knows is picking us up. Mom's all excited for me. She says it'll be good for me to make new friends."

"What's wrong with your old ones?" Jon asked in mock seriousness. "What'd I ever do to Annie?"

"She thinks you're gay," Neil laughed. "Talk to you tomorrow."

Ninety minutes later, Neil stood in the entranceway of Thorne's expansive and expensive house. The party was already in full swing. Indecipherable rock music blared from a stereo, while dozens of East Hill students milled about in Thorne's sunken living room.

Neil knew most of the kids by sight, if not by name. They were girls and guys from his classes or ones he'd seen in the lunchroom, but here at the party – clutching cigarettes and cans of beer, instead of pens and milk cartons – they seemed strangely out of context to him. Scanning the crowded living room looking for a friendly face, Neil finally spotted Dave Cavenall at the wet bar.

"See you later," Neil said to Marc, before looking around to see that his brother had already left him and disappeared into the crowd. Neil made a beeline towards Dave, before his teammate melted into the crowd, as well.

"Hey, Neil, what's shakin'?" Dave asked, when Neil finally squeezed his way to the bar. "You look thirsty. How 'bout a beverage?"

"Sure, uhhh…what do you got?" inquired Neil, asking not because he wanted to know what his options were, but because he didn't know any drink names and wouldn't be able to place an order unless he heard one.

"I can make you a Screwdriver, a Margarita, a rum and Coke, a…"

"Rum and coke sounds good," interrupted Neil, figuring that at least this concoction included a soft drink he liked. I haven't had one of those lately (or ever)."

"Looks like we're out of Coke. Pepsi Light, okay?"

"Yeah, that's fine."

Executing a simultaneous two-handed pour from a bottle of Captain Morgan and a can of Pepsi Light into a drinking glass adorned with the characters from *Scooby Doo*, Dave handed the carbonated cocktail to Neil.

The first-time drinker took a sip and gagged, the bitter bite from the rum overwhelming the flavor of the lemon-flavored soft drink. Reacting as if the cocktail was of the Molotov variety, Neil's jaw clenched, neck muscles bulged and his eyes shut tight. *Either Dave's bartending skills leave a lot to be desired*, Neil thought, *or this was the worst drink ever invented.*

"You all right, Neil?" asked Dave, clapping the youth's back with an open hand.

"Yeah, I'm fine," coughed Neil. "It just went down the wrong pipe. You know, maybe I'll have a cold beer instead."

Dave ducked behind the bar, emerging a second later to thrust a can of Schaefer into Neil's hand.

Tugging the pull-tab off the lid, Neil looked around the room.

"Is there a trash basket around to put this in?" asked Neil, holding the tab like a ring on the end of his index finger.

"Nah, just stick it back in the can," said Dave dismissively. "Everybody drinks brew that way."

Thinking twice about the potential choking hazard of inserting the small, curled piece of aluminum back into a dark can from which he'd be drinking from, Neil instead slipped the pull-tab into the front pocket of his corduroys when Dave looked away.

"Drink up," instructed Dave. "Cheers."

Taking a swig from the first beer he'd tasted since his father had let him take sips from his mug when he was a toddler, Neil reacted like the beer can was filled with another rum and coke – mixed with the output of someone who was suffering from a urinary tract infection.

"No good?" asked Dave.

"Oh, no, it's fine," said Neil, as his eyes began to water. "This isn't my normal brand of beer, that's all."

"Whatever you say, Neil. You know people here, right?"

"Yeah, sure. A lot of people."

"Good. Check you later then, okay? Rock on, man."

"Okay, Dave."

Alone now in a sea of fellow classmates, Neil floated from room to room searching for his brother while nursing a beer that tasted worse the warmer it got. Drifting into the kitchen, Neil searched the cupboards until he found a plastic cup. Moving to the refrigerator, he found an ice cube tray in the freezer, scooped a handful of ice into the cup and proceeded to pour his can of beer over them.

"What are you doing?" asked Marc, suddenly appearing over Neil's shoulder.

"Putting some ice cubes in my beer," replied the naive Neil. "It tastes like piss. I thought getting it colder would improve the taste."

"This isn't soda. What's wrong with you? You don't put *ice cubes* in beer! Dump that shit out before somebody sees you and laughs you outta the party."

"Where've you been? I've been looking all over for you," asked Neil, furtively depositing the beer-soaked ice in the sink.

"Around," answered Marc evasively.

"You're not doing anything you shouldn't be doing, right?"

"Who are you, the cops? Is it okay with you if I have a beer?"

"Have mine, I'm done with it. How can you drink this stuff?"

"You get used to it."

"Who pays for all this, anyway?"

"Thorne and his sister, I guess. They have trust funds. Who cares who pays? Go have fun."

"I'd rather go home. When can we leave?"

"We just got here, Neil. Jesus H. Christ, you sound like Gerry when he goes shopping with mom. I've never heard someone at a party say that. If you don't wanna party, go find someplace to watch TV then."

"Where?"

"Try Thorne's room upstairs. He's got a big color set."

"You don't think he'd mind? The guy *hates* me. I really don't want to see him tonight, if I don't have to."

"Don't worry about it. His bedroom's probably the last place he'd go during a party. Plus, he's feelin' no pain. I just saw him outside gettin' high."

"Okay. Anything beats staying down here. I can't breathe with all this smoke around. Where is it?"

"Upstairs. Second door on the left, I think."

"Don't forget me, when you're ready to go. I don't wanna be stuck here."

~~~

Neil climbed a spiral staircase to a deserted second floor. Tentatively pushing open Thorne's slightly ajar bedroom door, Neil found the room unoccupied. Shutting the door behind him to block out the noise and smoke from downstairs, he looked around the bedroom. A bikini-clad poster of *Sports Illustrated* swimsuit model Cheryl Tiegs decked one wall, while a life-sized poster of Queen lead singer Freddie Mercury loomed over the waterbed.

Cheryl invitingly smiled at Neil, but the pubescent teen only had eyes for the shimmering, sixteen-piece, blue drum kit that took up nearly half the room. One, that made his old, pre-used set look

206

like it came from a landfill. Before he even walked over to check it out, Neil immediately recognized the kit as a Premier, an almost exact replica – right down to the two floor bass drums – of the one Keith Moon used during his tenure with the Who.

Sitting behind it on the drum stool, Neil looked over a kit that unfolded before him in waves of cymbals and hanging tom-toms. Neil always knew his bare bones kit was small, but Thorne's drum set was more than twice the size of his own. Two rows of mounted tom-toms were arranged in a semi circle from left to right and hanging above them loomed four crash cymbals. There looked to be more drums and cymbals than anyone short of Moon himself could hit. Someone could play blindfolded on it, Neil figured, and still make contact on a skin or a cymbal with nearly every swing of a drumstick.

Neil picked up the drumsticks resting on the snare and simulated playing – going through his limited repertoire of fills, before breaking off into a Moon impersonation and pretending to thrash about the kit. Shutting his eyes, Neil lost himself in the moment as he flailed away, opening them half a minute later to find Thorne standing before him.

"Hey, man. What're you doing?" asked Thorne, holding a can of beer and staring at Neil through bloodshot slits for eyes.

"Oh, I…ahhh…just came in to watch TV and I saw your kit," exclaimed Neil nervously. "Don't worry, I didn't actually play your drums…I'll go."

"No, it's cool. You play?"

"Yeah, I have a kit at home, but it's nothing like this. This is…awesome. Looks just like…"

"Keith Moon's, right?"

"Yeah. Where'd you get it? Musta been expensive. How much was it?"

"I dunno. The 'rents got it for me when I turned thirteen. Wanna play it?"

"Really? No, I wouldn't wanna make a lot of noise…with the party going on."

Thorne turned around and gently closed the bedroom door.

"Don't worry about it," said Thorne. "No one can hear anything from up here. Go ahead, play."

Neil proceeded to pound out a 4/4 time signature on the hi-hat and snare and execute a few soft fills. But feeling self-conscious with Thorne hovering over him, he stopped after about thirty seconds and set the sticks back down on the snare.

"Is that it?" Thorne asked, when Neil finished. "You can keep playing if you want."

"No, that's okay. This is such a nice kit, seems almost too perfect to even play on. I wouldn't wanna nick a rim, or anything."

"You're pretty good. Take lessons?"

"Nah. The little I know, I picked up by playing along to Who tapes."

"You're a Who fan? Me, too. Ever seen 'em in concert?"

"No. Even if my folks woulda let me go, tickets are so expensive. I don't have the money. You?"

"Twice. Remember when they played five dates at the Garden in September? Some buddies and I went to the first and last shows."

"*You* saw them in Madison Square Garden?! I read the reviews about them in the papers. They were some great concerts."

"I don't remember much. We were so wasted. Almost as baked as I am now."

Uncomfortable with the direction their talk seemed to be taking, the sober Neil picked up the drumsticks again and twirled them uneasily between his fingers. Perhaps sensing the growing tension in the room, Thorne changed the subject.

"Seen some of the chicks here tonight?" asked Thorne. "There's a lotta mamas with nice squeeze boxes, if you know what I mean."

"I hadn't really noticed," shrugged Neil, his cheeks blushing from embarrassment.

"Is Jon here?"

"Bischell? No. He couldn't make it."

"I guess you heard I'm back on the team, right? So, when're you coming back to bunt for us again?"

Same old Thorne, Neil thought. Disappointed at himself for letting his guard down and thinking for a moment that his longtime rival might not be that bad of a guy after all, Neil rose from the drum stool and started for the bedroom door.

"Hey, I was just messin' with you," said Thorne, moving towards the door as if to block it. "I didn't mean nothin' by it. Wanna take a look at my record collection, Neil?"

"Um…okay," said Neil warily, trying to recall if Thorne had ever called him by his first name before.

Thorne led Neil towards a bookshelf packed tightly with albums.

"I have every Who record they've ever made," boasted Thorne proudly, pulling out the band's famed 1969 rock opera album, *Tommy*. Ever heard this?"

"Lots of times. The movie was just on TV a few weeks ago."

"Next time it's on, come over and watch it."

"Yeah, maybe."

"'Pinball Wizard's' a cool song. I love the lyric *'That deaf, dumb and black boy, sure plays a mean pinball.'*"

"You mean *'deaf, dumb and <u>blind</u> boy.'*"

"Whatever."

Thorne chugged the rest of his beer, let out a loud belch, then slid out a record from the jacket of the double album. Walking

210

over to the stereo, he pressed the power button and gently placed the vinyl disk on the turntable, waited for the record to drop to the platter and carefully lowered the tone arm over the track he wanted. After hearing the initial crackling of needle meeting record, Neil recognized "See Me, Feel Me," from the first two notes. Were the Who's music ever exclusively featured in an episode of *Name That Tune*, Neil would probably be able to name every one of their selections faster than even Pete Townshend, the group's musical arranger and primary songwriter.

See me, feel me, touch me, heal me

"My favorite song," said Neil, talking over Roger Daltrey's relaxed, pleading vocals and Townsend's soaring harmonizing.

"Sit over here, close to the speaker," insisted Thorne. "You'll hear it better."

Neil did as he was told, parking himself on the edge of Thorne's black and white, checkered waterbed.

"One of my favorites, too," uttered Thorne softly, as he sat next to Neil. "This and 'Behind Blue Eyes.' I play that one so much, I've gone through two *Who's Next's* in the last six months."

See me, feel me, touch me, heal me

Neil shut his eyes to let his sense of hearing soak in the music. As he did, Thorne – fueled by liquid and weed encouragement – inched closer, dropping his hand spider-like onto Neil's right thigh. The hand crawled slowly up Neil's leg toward his groin, but he didn't dare open his eyes, afraid to confirm what his sense of touch was telling him.

See me, feel me, touch me, heal me

Neil's body stiffened. Every nerve ending stood at attention, as high as the volume of the song. Confused and uncomfortable, Neil started to recite the "Our Father" to himself before regaining his wits, changing course and rattling off a quick, but desperate, prayer to ask God to deliver him from his bad dream.

The prayer went unanswered. Neil felt the warmth of hot beer breath run down his collar, followed a split second later by Thorne's lips on his neck. Neil's heart was now beating so loudly that he could barely hear the tempo of the music build.

See me, feel me, touch me, heal meeeeeee

When the chorus started, Neil wanted to sing out in protest to Thorne, but his vocal chords were as paralyzed as the rest of his body.

Listening to you I get the music
Gazing at you I get the heat
Following you I climb the mountain
I get excitement at your feeeeeet

Finally, as Thorne's hand climbed into Neil's front pocket, Neil busted out of his shell, much like Tommy, the deaf, dumb and blind boy from the rock opera, when the character broke free from his unreceptive state.

"What're you doing?!" Neil demanded, as he moved off the bed. "Get off me!"

Right behind you I see the millions

"What? I thought you wanted it," asked a puzzled Thorne. "I know you're…"

On you I see the glory

"Gay? No, I'm not!" objected Neil, turning hurriedly to the door.

From you I get opinions
From you I get the storyyyy

"Get back here, man," cried Thorne, grabbing Neil by the back of his plaid, flannel shirt. "This didn't just happen. Understand?"

"Lemme go!" yelled Neil, trying to break away from Thorne's grip.

Listening to you I get the music

"No, not 'til you say this didn't happen."

Gazing at you I get the heat

"Stop it!"

Following you I climb the mountain
I get excitement at your feeeeet

Tackling Neil to the floor, Thorne began wailing away wildly at the back of Neil's head with a furious combination of rapid-fire punches that practically kept time to Moon's frenzied drum beats on the still-playing record.

Right behind you I see the millions
On you I see the glory
From you I get opinions
From you I get the storyyyy

"*Say* this *didn't* happen!" repeated Thorne angrily, his blue eyes bulging with rage, as he rained blows on the prone and helpless Neil. Too preoccupied with self-preservation to speak, Neil could only lay there defenselessly, trying in vain to protect his face with his hands, while Thorne's fists – one of which now held the beer pull-tab that had been in Neil's pocket – repeatedly connected with his victim's forearms and temples.

Listening to you I get the music
Gazing at you I get the heat
Following you I climb the mountain
I get excitement at your feet

Punching until he had nothing left to strike with, an exhausted Thorne dropped his tired, heavy arms and slumped backwards. Peeking tentatively from behind his closed, nicked hands, Neil seized the opportunity to escape, wriggled out from under Thorne and bolted from the room. Glancing over his shoulder for fear that Thorne might be giving chase, Neil barreled down the stairs faster than if he was trying to steal a base on a ball field. Pushing his way through the crowd in the living room, head down, Neil attracted infinitely more attention on his way out of the party than he did when making his entrance.

"Watch it, kid!" cried an angry partygoer, looking over his beer-soaked shirt following an accidental collision with Neil.

Pressing forward, Neil reached the front door and flung it open. As he was about to race outside, Neil felt a strong tug on his arm.

214

Afraid that Thorne had caught up to him and was ready for round two of their fight, Neil turned his face away and braced himself to be hit again.

"Neil, what the hell's goin' on?" asked Marc, looking over his brother's face, puffy and black and blue from Thorne's fists and nicked and bleeding from the sharp end of the pull-tab.

"Th…Thorne," stammered a breathless Neil. "He was touching me…I told him to stop… and then he started pounding on me."

"Wait a minute! Slow down. Say that again."

"I was in his room…he came in…we were talking and listening to music and outta nowhere he comes onto me…touching me, kissing me. I tried to leave and he tackled me and started punching me. When he stopped, I ran out."

"What? Why would he do that?"

"You think I'm making this up, Marc? Then you tell me why he did this! You know him better than I do! I gotta get outta here."

Breaking loose from Marc's grip, Neil turned, ran from the house, high hurtled a row of hedges lining the front stoop and disappeared into the darkness.

"Neil, wait!" Marc called out to his brother. "I'll get us a ride home. Neil!" NEILLL!"

Rushing back into the house, Marc pushed his way through the crowd and climbed the stairs two at a time to the second floor.

"Hey, Bobby, why'd you beat up my brother?" asked a miffed Marc, finding the party host lying face up on his bed.

"What brother?!" snorted Thorne. "I don't know your *brother*."

"Neil Bricker…the kid you just beat the crap out of. *He's* my brother."

"The little white kid?!"

"Yeah. His folks adopted me; he's my brother. Why'd you do that to him?"

"Sorry to tell you, man, but your brother's a faggot; he tried to kiss me, so I taught him a lesson."

"No. I know my own brother and he wouldn't do that."

Thorne rose from the bed and brushed past Marc, out of the bedroom and into the hallway.

"You're a liar, Bobby," said Marc, from behind, refusing to let the argument die.

"Believe it," countered Thorne, wheeling around to confront Marc. "Jose *Queer*vo, tried to kiss me. Your brother's a fuckin' faggot!"

"No, he's not. That's not cool. Neil's not here to defend himself."

"Well, the little faggot couldn't defend himself when he was here, either."

CHAPTER 18

Standing in for his absent brother, Marc bull rushed Thorne, now with his back turned, to the floor at the top of the hallway stairs – the commotion attracting the attention of some of the partygoers on the floor below. Gaining the upper hand from the start, Marc pinned Thorne, sat his knees on the boy's elbows and began to batter him wildly about the head with slaps and punches. Like Neil, minutes earlier, all Thorne could do was cover up his face and play defense, but unlike Neil, Thorne was fortunate to have his beating take place in front of friends. Moments after the fight began, a handful of classmates came to Thorne's defense, separating the two.

Picking himself off the floor, Thorne lightly fingered his face. Finding blood on his hand, he advanced on Marc, who was still being held down by a half dozen teens.

"You fucking nigger!" cried Thorne, balling his right hand into a fist and delivering a downward blow that caved in the right side of his victim's face.

As blood spurted from Marc's mouth onto his white polo shirt, Thorne continued beating his stationary target about the head with alternating hard left and right hands.

"Stop it, man!" cried Marc.

"Not 'til you say 'uncle', Buckwheat," laughed Thorne maniacally, now working his fists into Marc's stomach and ribs. "Say 'Uncle Tom.' Say it."

"Unc...Uncle," gasped Marc, fighting with the only weapon he had left, his tongue, to hold onto a dignity Thorne was determined to steal from him.

"No, 'Uncle TOM!'" insisted Thorne, punching once more with extra emphasis.

"Okay...okay, uncle...Uncle Tom," cried Marc, no longer able to withstand the suffering.

Finally satisfied with Marc's answer, Thorne stopped punching and started to rise from the floor, shoving two hands into Marc's chest for leverage to push himself up.

Released by Thorne's friends, Marc slowly turned over onto his hands and knees, coughing violently; a thin stream of bloody spittle dripping from his mouth.

"Get Buckwheat outta here before he spews all over the floor," said Thorne, drawing laughs from the large crowd of onlookers, who'd gathered to watch the fight.

Like a maitre d' snapping his fingers to summon a busboy to clear off a table, the same group of friends quickly heeded his call, scooped up Marc and physically removed the battered boy from the house.

Too exhausted and beaten up to resist, Marc now lay sprawled on his back on the stoop – the *Commodores'* song "Sail On" seeping through the closed front door and into his ears – and stared as if in a trance at the clear night sky, trying to piece together what had just happened.

A few minutes earlier, he'd been enjoying himself, just as he'd been at school parties nearly every weekend for the past eight months. Now, suddenly, he'd been harshly kicked to the popularity curb, discarded like a crushed and empty beer can.

With his ride home still partying inside and apparently disinterested in his condition, Marc accepted that the only way back to Eastham – some three miles away – was by foot. Staggering to his feet, jaw swelling and ribs aching, Marc started walking stiffly and slowly, following the path his brother forged minutes earlier. Two short streets later, Marc headed east along Woodbridge Lane, a two-mile stretch of lonely, sidewalk-less road that fed into Eastham.

~~~

Nearly a mile up the same road, an exhausted Neil finally decided it was safe to stop running. Absent a sidewalk, Neil hiked home along the two-lane road's dirt shoulder – facing traffic – thinking he'd be better able to sidestep an oncoming car than one approaching him from the rear.

It was now 10:00 p.m. and with street lights spaced few and far between and houses set well off the road behind a thick cover of tall trees and brush, Neil felt like he was walking through a dark tunnel. It was the type of road he'd normally be afraid to navigate even during broad daylight. But Neil was too distressed and shell-shocked about what had happened at the party to give his creepy surroundings much thought. Primary on Neil's mind was to get home as soon as possible, scrub his neck where Thorne had kissed it, then apply an ice pack to the growing knot on the right side of his forehead, before crawling into bed and curling up in the fetal position to try and sleep away the night's bad memory.

Yards shy of the Eastham town line, a car drove out of a side street and pulled up alongside Neil.

"Out a little late tonight, aren't you, son?" asked a man from behind a glowing flashlight in an almost avuncular tone. "Where you headed?"

"Just on my way home, officer," said Neil politely, after reading to himself 'Woodbridge, N.J. Police' imprinted in white letters over a 2' x 1' image of a black badge painted onto the passenger side of the marked car.

"Where do you live?"

"Eastham."

"Visiting friends in Woodbridge, were you?"

"Yes, sir."

"Want a lift home?"

"No, thank you. I don't live too far from here."

"Okay. Have a good night."

Pulling back on the road, the police car continued heading west.

That was a close call, thought Neil. While he'd only had a little to drink that night, the cop would have undoubtedly smelled alcohol on his breath had he bothered to get out of his car and talk to Neil up close.

A minute later, the same police officer who stopped Neil rounded a bend and came upon Marc. Parking his car about ten feet in front of the youth, the officer flashed on the high beams, turned off the ignition and exited the vehicle.

"You know it's about ten minutes past the 11:00 curfew, right?" the cop asked coldly, his right hand resting on his holstered revolver as he walked cautiously toward Marc.

"No, I didn't know that. I'm sorry, officer, I lost track of time," said an amenable Marc, shielding his eyes from the car's intense light.

"Where were you tonight?"

"A party."

"Have you been drinking?"

"Ahhh…just a little."

"How old are you?"

"Fifteen."

"Even a little's too much for someone who's underage. You seem kinda tall to be fifteen."

"What else have you been up to tonight?" inquired the cop, pointing to Marc's rumpled, blood-spattered shirt.

"Nothin'," answered Marc nervously, with a shrug of his shoulders. "I just got into a little fight."

221

"Uh-huh. Musta been some party. You don't live around here, do you?"

"No…well, I live in Eastham. I go to East Hill High School."

"Right. I don't suppose you have an ID on you."

"No, I left my school ID at home. But really, I live in Eastham. My name is Marc Harper and I'm a freshman at East…"

"But without ID how do I know that? C'mon."

Grabbing Marc firmly by the elbow, the officer, who was about four inches shorter, but forty pounds heavier than the gangly teenager, began to escort the boy to his squad car.

"What are you doing? All I did was have a beer tonight," said a confused Marc. "Am I under arrest for something?"

"Nope," the officer answered, "but I wanna find out who you are, so we're gonna make a trip to the station."

"Let go of me, man, I'm coming, I'm coming."

The cop stopped walking and turned to Marc.

"Listen, it's up to you. We can do this the easy way or the hard way," said the officer, ensuring his message was received by applying more pressure to Marc's elbow. "You're in enough trouble as it is. You're wandering around a strange town at night, with unaccounted for blood on you. And either you've lied to me about your age or you're underage drinking – and violating curfew."

"But it's my blood."

"Get in the car and clam up."

Opening the door to the back seat, the cop pushed Marc into the converted Dodge Monaco, dropped into the driver's seat, started the engine and pulled out onto the dark road.

Through the heavy wire mesh partition separating the front from the rear row of the cruiser, Marc's eyes fixated on the imposing, semiautomatic shotgun mounted upright near the dashboard.

~~~

"What you got there, Mikey?" asked the desk sergeant, looking up from his paperback, when the patrolman led Marc into the Woodbridge Police Station two minutes later.

"I dunno yet, Frank," the officer said. "Found him on Woodbridge Road…beer on his breath…blood on his shirt…says he's fifteen and lives in Eastham but he got no ID. Thought I'd bring him in and see if his story checks out."

The sergeant put down his book, rose from his chair, walked back to an office and emerged a minute later with a Breathalyzer.

"First, let's see how much this guy had to drink tonight," said the sergeant, talking through the dead cigar clenched between his teeth. "Blow into this."

"What's this do?" Marc asked.

"It measures your blood alcohol level. Quit stalling and blow."

223

Wrapping his lips around the plastic tube sticking out from the calculator-sized Breathalyzer, Marc drew in and took a healthy puff.

"Let's see," said the farsighted sergeant, turning the Breathalyzer back to him before straightening out his elbow to get a better view of the numbers printed on the instrument. "Your blood alcohol level is .02%."

"Is that okay?" asked Marc.

"It means you're not legally intoxicated. However, you're not out of the woods. If you *are* only fifteen, as you say you are, you still shouldn't be drinking. The minimum age for alcohol consumption in the state of New Jersey is eighteen. So, if you're fifteen, you'd be in violation of this law. Wanna tell us where you were drinking tonight?"

"A house party."

"And where was this alleged house party?"

"I don't know the street name."

"I'll bet. Park it on the bench for a minute."

Marc's minute on the long, wooden bench that ran across the front wall of the stationhouse stretched to ten and then fifteen – his nervousness growing exponentially with every passing minute.

"Over here," said the officer who brought Marc in, finally appearing in the doorway of a room twenty feet away and gesturing with his index finger.

Jumping off the bench, Marc entered the sparsely decorated room, an exposed light bulb from the ceiling hanging over a cheap-looking wooden table and two metal folding chairs.

"Call your folks," said the cop, matter of factly. "Tell them where you are and to come and get you."

Marc fumbled nervously with the receiver of the phone on the table, gathered himself and paused.

"What's the matter?" asked the officer, sounding annoyed.

"I...I... forgot my phone number," stuttered Marc.

"Now, I've heard everything."

Leaving the room, the snickering officer returned a few seconds later with a copy of the Bergen County white pages telephone book.

"Will you need help dialing, too?" asked the officer, tossing the thick directory on the table in front of Marc.

Thumbing through the book, Marc found the Bricker's listing, picked up the phone again and dialed the number.

"Ah...Bricker residence...Al speaking," said a groggy-sounding Al, answering the phone on the second ring.

"Dad, it's me," Marc said.

"Me, who?"

"Marc."

"Where are you?"

"I'm at the Woodbridge Police Station. I need you to come and get me."

"Marc, what's goin' on?" Al asked, the words "police station" having snapped the lethargic man into full consciousness. "Are you okay?"

"I'm okay, dad. I'll tell you when you get here."

"What street's it on?"

"I dunno."

"Never mind, I think I know where it is. I'll be right there."

Leaping out of bed, Al pulled on the first pair of pants he saw – his dirty trousers draped over the clothes hamper – and exited the bedroom without stirring Ann, who'd been sleeping soundly next to him. Moments later in the kitchen, Al was zipping a windbreaker over his t-shirt when Neil walked in the back door.

"Dad?! What are you doing up?" exclaimed a startled Neil, not expecting to see his father awake and fully dressed at that hour.

CHAPTER 19

"Where the hell were you guys tonight?" demanded Al, glaring at Neil, but apparently not noticing the cuts and red puffiness on his son's face.

"We went to the movies, remember?"

"Oh, are they showing movies at the Woodbridge Police Department now?"

"Huh?"

"Your brother just called from jail. I'm going to pick him up."

Brushing past Neil and out the door, Al hopped into the VW and started it up – putting the bus into drive just as Neil climbed into the front passenger seat.

"We went to a house party in Woodbridge," Neil confessed.

"Wonderful," said Al sarcastically, barreling the bus out of the driveway. "So, how'd your brother land in jail?"

"Beats me. Honest. I left early and walked home."

Four silent miles later, Al pulled the VW into the parking lot of the Woodbridge Police Station.

"Where's my son?!" asked Al, barely through the doors of the stationhouse before he blurted out the question.

"Who's your son, sir?" the desk sergeant inquired with a quizzical look.

"Marc Harper. He called five minutes ago and said he was here."

"The black kid? But you're…"

"White? Yeah, how'd you tell? What's my son doing here?"

"Take it easy, sir. Calm down. What's your name?"

"Al Bricker. I live at 15 Grove Street in Eastham."

"And a Marc Harper is your son?"

"Yes!"

"Okay, just a minute, sir. Wait right here."

Disappearing into the station's interrogation room, the sergeant soon resurfaced with his fellow officer and Marc, looking scared, far younger and far smaller than his fifteen years and 6'4" height would suggest.

"Is this your son, Mr. Bricker?" asked the sergeant.

"Yes, that's him," Al said. "What'd he do?"

"How old is he?"

"He's fifteen. Now, will you please tell me what happened?"

"Officer Molinski here found him roaming around on Woodbridge Road. He had blood on him, that he said came from a fistfight, and he admitted drinking at a party, so we gave him a Breathalyzer test and he tested positive. We'll release him into your custody, Mr. Bricker, but I suggest you have a talk with him about underage drinking; I trust this won't happen again."

"No, it won't, officer. *Will it*, Marc?"

"No," answered Marc, head down, in a barely audible voice.

"Let's go," Al said.

"Hey, didn't I just see you a little while ago?" asked Officer Molinski, as the Brickers turned to walk out the front door of the stationhouse.

"Uhhh…yes…that was me," answered Neil sheepishly.

"What!? You were stopped too, Neil?" Al asked. "What'd *you* do?"

"The officer stopped me while I was walking home from the party," said Neil.

"Were *you* in a fight tonight, too?" Al wondered aloud, finally noticing the scrapes and bruises on Neil's face. "With who? Marc?"

"Yes, but not with Marc."

"Were you drinking, too?"

"I had about half a beer."

"So, why didn't you bring him down here, as well?" asked Al, looking incredulously at Officer Molinski, while pointing a thumb at Neil. "He did everything my other son did."

"Sir, I brought your other son in because in my judgment there was something not right about his appearance," replied the patrolman.

"Was it because his appearance is black?"

"I didn't say that, sir."

"You didn't have to."

"Mr. Bricker, we have an obligation to the taxpayers of this community…"

"To what," Al interrupted, "keep the Woodbridge streets safe from a benign fifteen year old, who happens to live in the next town over? Spare me the speech. I've heard it before. I know the routine. You see a black kid by himself at night and assume he's up to no good. You'll take any excuse that gives you a break from being a full-time meter maid."

Pushing open the station's front door, Al stormed out, followed by Neil and Marc.

"Get in the damn car!" Al hollered at his sons.

Too upset to speak anymore, Al didn't say another word to the pair until he'd pulled into the family's driveway and parked the car.

"We'll talk about this tomorrow with your mother," said Al, slamming the stick on the transmission from "drive" to "park" so violently that it threatened to break off in his massive hand. "Guess I don't have to tell you you're both indefinitely grounded on weekends, do I?"

~~~

Trudging despondently into the house and then up to their bedroom, Neil and Marc quietly undressed in the dark, so as not wake their little brother.

"Marc, what happened at the party after I left," whispered Neil, after the two had slipped into their respective beds. "Who'd *you* get into a fight with?"

"Your friend, Bobby," Marc answered softly.

"No way."

"I asked him why he beat on you and he said it was because you tried to kiss him. Told him he was a liar and we got into it. Next thing I knew, some kids were holding me down, so Thorne could use me for a punching bag."

"Wow. So, you didn't believe what he said about me?"

"I know you're not gay; and I didn't want him saying you were."

"Then what happened?"

"They threw me out and I started walking home…until that cop picked me up."

"Were you scared? I woulda been..."

"How's your face?"

"I feel like there's a tumor growing outta my forehead and I cut myself shaving in fifty places. How's yours feel?"

"The same."

"What were you thinking when that cop stopped you?"

"I'm tired, Neil. Can we talk about this tomorrow?"

"Sure. Ummm...?"

"Uh-huh."

"Thanks for standing up for me, especially, when you didn't have to. That took a lotta guts."

"Well, I learned a lot tonight."

"Like what?"

Marc inhaled to his toes and exhaled his reply.

"Like...how I don't fit in here as much as I thought and how I'll *never* fit in here," he continued.

"Hey, don't let one jerk change your mind," reassured Neil. "You've got tons of friends besides Thorne."

"That's what I thought, but it's more than just the fight. It's what went down during it. Thorne kept calling me…Buckwheat…Uncle Tom…and nigger…and not *one* person stopped him. They just laughed or held me down so he could keep hitting me."

Jumping out of his top bunk, Neil made his way across the dark bedroom and took a seat on the floor by the head of Marc's bed.

"What the hell?!" Neil exclaimed. "Why would he say that?"

"Because 'nigger's' always on the tips of white people's tongues," Marc answered. "Ready to say to put us back in our place."

"That's not true. You know we'd never talk to you like that. Mom and dad taught us to *never* use that word. I think I'd get into less trouble if I called Gerry a shithead or a little fucker than if I called a black person a nig…see, I can't even say it."

"It *is* true, Neil. Don't be so naive. I had a lotta time to think in that police station. It doesn't matter whether you say it or not, you still think it – all white people do. That cop never called me a nigger, but he treated me like one."

Marc stopped talking and turned his head to the right to look out the window at the late-night sky.

"It's kinda funny," Marc continued, a moment later, still gazing out the glass.

"What is?" asked Neil.

"In all the years I've lived here, not *one* person's ever called me a 'nigger' to my face; I'd almost forgotten the word existed."

"That's good, isn't it?"

"No. It was just false security. I know Al and Ann mean well, but now I know they didn't do me any favors adopting me. I got tricked into thinking all white people are like your family and they're not. The rest of the world isn't colorblind. Your folks didn't teach me how to deal with that. They can't raise me right."

"What do you mean *not* raise you right?" asked Neil, taken aback by Marc's remarks and from never before hearing his brother refer to his parents by their first names. "They're raising you the same way they're raising the rest of us."

"That's what I mean. They can't raise me to be a black man. They can only raise me to be a white guy from the suburbs. Me being here isn't helping Al and Ann much, either."

"How's that?"

"Have you noticed they don't have as many friends as they used to? They almost never go out to parties anymore."

"That's because mom went back to school and they don't have as much time…"

"No, it's because of me. *Twice* last summer at barbeques at the lake I overheard Ann telling Al about somebody who told her they didn't think it was a good idea that they took me in…and those are just the ones I know about. Who knows how many other people told them the same thing?"

"Okay, but those were probably just people they only knew a little bit. Knowing dad he could probably care less. He probably blew it off and told mom 'it's one less family we don't have to waste a stamp on when we send out Christmas cards.'"

"Nope. One family was the O'Connells. Al's known Mr. O.C. since they were kids. Mr. O.C. hasn't been here in months and he used to come over for coffee every Saturday morning. And Ann and Mrs. V. C. were best friends. They used to carpool together to Fordham, take guitar lessons together...go to Tupperware parties. Not anymore.

"Right now, I wish I'd never left Paterson. At least in the projects I knew who I was. But now I've lived here too long to go back. I don't belong *here* and I don't fit *there*. I'd fit in there now about as well as you would.

"Except for that argument you and I had awhile back, tonight was the first time since that Cabbage Night a couple years ago that I was really reminded I'm black. I mean...I always know it, but until tonight with the fight and then the cop stopping me, it didn't seem like anyone else knew it or cared. It just shows that no matter what I do, or how many friends I have, it comes down to one thing: I'll always be nothing more than a nigger here."

Marc paused and shook his head in disbelief.

"Marc?" he wondered aloud. "What kind of a name is that for a black guy? You know, my mother named me Marcus after my grandfather. She always said he had the strongest character of any man she ever knew. Faced every kind of discrimination growing up in Alabama, but was always proud of who he was. Marc?! Man, what the hell was I thinking?"

"I don't know what to say."

"There's nothing you can say. Consider yourself lucky, Neil. You'll never know what it's like to be black and to live here."

"Yeah, I'm *really* lucky. At least you *have* fit in. I've *never* fit in at East Hill and after tonight, I never will. Thorne'll tell everyone I'm gay and they'll all believe it. You *know* what my life's gonna be like in school from now on? It'll be worse than it already is. At least before I was invisible there. Now, I'll have to put up with people's crap for three more years because mom and dad already said I can't transfer to St. Rita's. There's no way I'll ever live this down."

"I know. Looks like we're both gonna have to get used to living with prejudice. Things won't be the same anymore."

"You know what I was thinking about the other day?" said Neil wistfully. "Remember that time we were at the lake, that first summer you were here? We were swimming, trying to see who could hold their breath underwater the longest. I always wanted to know what your afro felt like, so I reached out and squeezed it. Then you did the same thing to my hair. Remember that?"

"Yeah, I remember. That water was always so gross and green. It was like Ann's pea soup. What *did* my hair feel like?"

"Like a brown, foam basketball."

"What did mine feel like?"

"Wet straw."

"I guess I just wanted to know what it would be like to be you. Before we met, I thought every black kid was like the ones in the *Fat Albert* cartoons."

"And I thought all white people were like those on *Little House on the Prairie* or *The Waltons*. Then when I got here, it *was* like *The Waltons*. There were so many crickets at night that I couldn't sleep. I needed some police sirens and street noise to relax me and put me out."

Ten seconds of silence passed between the two brothers.

"Well, good night, Neil Boy," said Marc.

"Good night, Marc Boy," snickered Neil, climbing back onto his bunk.

"Marcus."

CHAPTER 20

"Who's there?" asked Neil, jolted from a light sleep thirty minutes later by the squeak of the rusty hinges on his bedroom door.

"It's just me, Neil," whispered Marc. "Go back to sleep."

"Marc? Marcus? Where you going?" asked Neil, propping himself up on his elbows to catch sight of his fully-clothed brother bathed in the light of a full moon streaming through their bedroom window.

"I can't sleep. I'm going out for a walk."

"Wait up. I'll come with you."

"No. I wanna be alone."

"But what about the curfew? You don't wanna get stopped again. Dad's gonna be *really* pissed if he has to pick you up at another police station tonight."

"Don't worry about it. He won't."

"Okay, but stay off the main streets, just in case."

Fully awake now, Neil began to think and worry about the consequences of that night's events. An hour later – still unable to sleep – he, too, got out of bed, dressed and slipped out of the house.

~~~

A jogger found the body early the next morning – mistaking it at first for a dummy hung in effigy as a high school prank – hanging from the east goal post on the East Hill football field, silhouetted against the rising sun. Two days later, his death was announced over the loudspeakers at the school's morning announcements.

The untimely passing of a peer was all the East Hill student body could talk about that day. And when word got out about the cause of death, more questions than answers were raised. Why, went the common cry, would a good looking, popular athlete like Bobby Thorne, who seemingly had everything going for him, drive his sister's Corvette to the high school and take his own life? It didn't add up. Maybe, it was speculated, he had problems at home, or was too high or drunk from a night of heavy partying to think clearly about what he was doing.

Thorne's suicide especially gnawed at Neil. Unable to eat a full meal, the teen dropped five pounds in the ensuing days and suffered from insomnia – the few moments of sleep he was able to grab a night haunted by nightmares of Thorne's clammy, groping hands.

The day before Thorne's funeral, a rainstorm washed out Neil's jayvee baseball game. Following yet another day of brooding in public, Neil retreated to his bedroom after school to mope in private. Pausing for a moment from vacantly watching the rain pelt against the window, without thinking Neil popped *Who's Next* into his tape player before resuming his lost staring.

Over roughly the next half hour, one Who song after another – from "Baba O'Riley," "The Song is Over," and "Going Mobile" absent mindedly went in one of Neil's ears and out the other.

The eighth track on the nine-song tape – "Behind Blue Eyes" – opened with a slow guitar riff. As if hearing the music for the first time that day, Neil instantly recalled the feelings Thorne had expressed to him about that song on the night of the fateful party: *I play that one so much, I've gone through two* Who's Next's *in the last six months.*

A second later, Roger Daltrey's gently spoken, forlorn lyrics interrupted Neil's thoughts.

No one knows what it's like
To be the bad man
To be the sad man
Behind blue eyes

No one knows what it's like
To be hated
To be fated
To telling only lies

But my dreams
They aren't as empty
As my conscience seems to be

I have hours, only lonely
My love is vengeance
That's never free

No one knows what it's like
To feel these feelings
Like I do
And I blame you

No one bites back as hard on their anger

240

None of my pain and woe can show through

But my dreeeaaams
They aren't as empty
As my conscience seems to be

I have hours, only lonely
My love is vengeance
That's never freeeeee

As the song was about to launch into its next verse, it suddenly took on an edgier tone – complete with power chords on electric guitar, rapid-fire drumming and sneering singing.

When my fist clenches, crack it open
Before I use it and lose my cool
When I smile please tell me some bad news
Before I laugh and act like a fool

If I swallow anything evil put your finger down my throat
And if I shiver please give me a blanket
Keep me warm, let me wear your coat

"Behind Blue Eyes" then slipped back to its slow, tormented tempo for the final chorus.

No one knows what it's like
To be the bad man
To be the sad man
Behind blue eyes

Neil had heard "Behind Blue Eyes" hundreds of times, but until now he'd never really paid much attention to the lyrics. More often than not, he'd be listening to the song while playing drums, impatiently waiting out or fast-forwarding past the first few slow, quiet verses, until reaching the spot on the song when drums were required.

But today – depressed and sapped of the energy needed to play on his kit – Neil allowed himself to listen and process the song, feeling as if he'd discovered an entirely new piece of music, whose lyrics were speaking directly to him.

Like a wartime cryptographer, meticulously trying to crack the enemy's code, Neil rewound and listened to the song a half dozen more times, analyzing and interpreting the lyrics in hopes of making sense of Thorne's life. By the last replay, Neil no longer heard Daltrey's voice, but Thorne's – singing his secret to him from beyond the grave.

Thorne had adapted the meaning behind the lyrics to fit his lonely life, Neil concluded. No one knew what it was like to feel the pressure to be someone he wasn't, or the shame of a socially unacceptable sexual orientation, so Thorne hid from the woe behind a mountain of macho bravado, dulling the pain with drugs and alcohol; sports and bullying became the physical outlet by which he channeled his repressed feelings.

Few kids in school had more friends, but so afraid was he of the stigma attached to his homosexuality, Thorne apparently couldn't let even one of them in on his private life. Consequently, he had no one to crack open his clenched fist before he lost his cool; stick a finger down his throat to release his evil; or cover him with a blanket to comfort him. No one had any idea what it was like to be the bad, sad man behind Thorne's blue eyes.

Wrapping himself in the comforter off his bed, Neil shuddered hard at the thought that Thorne's party seduction was likely his clumsy attempt to connect with another lost – and presumably – homosexual soul.

Neil wondered whether Thorne – once his advance was rejected, and perhaps fearful that Neil would spill the beans about his homosexuality – decided that he could neither live a lie anymore nor face the truth. Life as a closet or an "outed" gay at a judgmental, status-oriented high school like East Hill for the next three years was apparently too heavy of a cross to bear, so he left it dangling from a cross bar on an empty football field.

~~~

The following morning, Neil and Molly – with Marcus begging off attending, citing a stomach bug – stood solemnly at the back of Woodbridge's packed and airless First Episcopal Church for Thorne's funeral. Even in death, Thorne was popular, marveled Neil to himself as he scanned the vast church. Not a vacant seat could be found and the church would have undoubtedly been in violation of the fire code had not the local fire marshal himself been there as a private citizen to pay his respects.

Neil still didn't like Thorne – or the cruel and vicious things he'd done to him – but he felt compelled to attend the funeral, if for no other reason than he now felt a kinship with the troubled youth. Moreover, Neil reasoned that he probably knew Thorne far better than any of the shell-shocked and grieving family and friends huddled in the church, still searching for answers to his death.

"Mr. and Mrs. Thorne," said Neil, nervously curling up the church program in his hands, as he approached Thorne's parents during a private moment in the cemetery following the funeral mass. "I just wanted to say how sorry I am about Thor…umm…Bobby."

"Thank you," said Mrs. Thorne through a tender half smile. "I don't believe we've met you before. Were you a friend of Bobby's?"

"Not really, but I knew Bobby from school. My name's Neil, I'm from Eastham. We were on the baseball team together."

"Bobby loved baseball. It was his favorite sport. We even put his mitt with him in the coff…"

Unable to finish her sentence, Mrs. Thorne turned to the elevated, veneer wood casket awaiting lowering into its dug out grave. Seeing the tears now pooling in her eyes, Neil wanted to say what he knew and suspected and give she and her husband some insight into their son's personal struggles.

But just as Neil was about to stammer out some words of consolation he thought better of it. How could knowing that their son was gay and couldn't deal with it, help lessen their grief, he thought? If anything, it might cause them even more hurt. Maybe it was better to let them believe that the marijuana and empty beer bottles found in the front seat of his sister's car were the main suspects in his death, instead of just accessories to it. Besides, what right did he have, Neil continued, to raze the carefully constructed house of cards and mirrors where Thorne housed his distorted self-image.

"He really knew how to play the game," said Neil, instead.

"Thank you for saying that," said Mrs. Thorne, applying a gentle, two-handed shake to Neil's right hand.

"Say, that's quite a shiner you got there?" said Mr. Thorne, noticing the healing, but still discolored left side of Neil's face.

"I got into a little disagreement with someone," answered Neil, raising a hand to cover the bruise.

"I hope you gave back as good as you got."

"Ummm…he got it much worse – worse than he deserved."

~~~

A day later, the jayvee team played its first game since Thorne's death – with no one on the squad looking forward to this symbolic return to normalcy more than Neil. Ever since he'd downed his first Gatorade, Neil had used sports as a release to escape his troubles. No matter what the problem, even if was with sports itself – as was the case when he failed to make the freshman basketball team – he could always depend on athletics to deliver him from a dilemma.

But as happy as he was to resume his season, Neil found it impossible to distance himself from the traumatic events of the past week. Only Neil's body took the field; his mind was on Marcus, the Bricker boathouse's new tenant, who'd taken to smoking dope there at night and after school, as a means to escape his feelings of isolation; and on Thorne, lying in a brand new, tailored suit in a cemetery some three miles away. They were the two peers in his life – regardless of his complicated feelings for them – who seemed to have the world on a string. Now, one was strung out and dying inside and the other dead by his own hand.

Neil's lack of concentration reflected in his poor performance that afternoon. At the plate, Neil struck out leading off the home half of the opening inning – fanning for just the first time all season – on a called strike meatball that he'd normally line up the middle for a single. Defensively, he was even worse. In center field, the distracted Neil continually lost track of pitch counts and outs and once threw to the wrong base after retrieving a base hit, allowing an opposing runner to score.

When the top of the third inning began, Neil's mind wandered from the past to his future. How long, he wondered, could sports be used as a crutch – or his drug of choice – to support his fragile self-esteem?

Thorne had excelled in *three* sports and yet his love for them wasn't strong enough to keep his demons at bay. Neil had just one sport left and its shelf life had an expiration date. Neil knew now that he was good enough to play organized baseball through high school, but what would happen after he graduated? What college or major league teams, he wondered, would be interested in a frail, spray hitter with a weak arm? Time was running out in his fantasy world; on the one thing he could do well; the *only* thing he really wanted to do in life.

Just then, a solid crack from an aluminum bat shook Neil from his stupor. As if shot out of a bazooka, a towering fly ball was hurtling toward him in straightaway center field. Climbing higher and higher, the ball easily crested the top of the soaring cedar trees that rose from the woods behind the backstop. Framed against the cobalt sky, Neil easily picked up the white sphere.

The pop fly was the kind he'd always loved to catch – high, soft and wafting directly to him. How great, Neil imagined, gliding in a few steps to line the ball up for the catch, if it just stayed there, stuck forever in a state of suspended, childhood bliss? His future was only bound to get harder and more complicated. Soon enough, life would be hitting him fewer and fewer easy fly balls. What was

246

so wrong with wanting to cherish and admire the poignancy of one?

"Take your time," Neil pleaded softly with the ball, as it finally began to peak. "I'll wait forever."

###

Made in the USA
Lexington, KY
13 July 2013